Paris, the city of light: an unexpected encounter

Eduardo Honorio Friaça

Copyright Notice

All rights in this book, including but not limited to the text, design, images, and graphics, are protected by copyright in accordance with Law No. 9,610/98, also known as the LDA (Copyright Law).

This book is a work of fiction and romance resulting from the author's creative and dedicated work. Any form of unauthorized reproduction, distribution , or use of the contents of this book, in whole or in part, without the express permission of the author, is strictly prohibited.

The author reserves all legal rights to protect his intellectual and creative property. The independent publication of this book in no way diminishes or compromises the author's copyright.

Any unauthorized use of this book, including copying, reproduction distribution, or public dissemination, will constitute copyright infringement and will be subject to appropriate legal action.

The author sincerely thanks all readers for their support and hopes they enjoy this original work of fiction. For usage requests or permissions, please contact the author.

Summary

In Search of New Perspectives

Luiz Schmitt Mancini is a renowned writer on the Brazilian literary scene. His fluid and poetic writing enchants readers of all ages and makes him one of the most promising authors of his generation. Mancini came from a family of Italian and German origin, which had immigrated to Brazil a few generations ago. He grew up in São Paulo, more precisely in the Higienópolis area, a noble and elegant district of the city. He spent most of his childhood there, in a penthouse overlooking the Pacaembu neighborhood.

Today, the writer still lives in the same penthouse and spends most of his time at home, writing his novels and short stories in his office. Luiz is known for his novels, such as Diary of an Alcoholic and Sloppy Girl. The writer even won awards for his work. However, he wasn't recognized worldwide.

Luiz's life in São Paulo is a rollercoaster of emotions. The city, known for its urban bustle and immense cultural diversity, provides fertile ground for Luiz's literary inspiration. He finds in the bustling streets, the architectural contrasts and the stories that each person carries with them an inexhaustible source of material for his creations.

Walking through the streets of São Paulo, Luiz is enchanted by the colonial architecture that dates back to the city's earliest days. The historic buildings, such as the Casa das Rosas and the São Bento Monastery, evoke an atmosphere of grandeur and cultural preservation. But he, a lover of tradition and classical aesthetics, is frustrated by the advance of the modern movement in São Paulo, which is destroying the city's architecture and beauty. The author, in the midst of the hustle and bustle of everyday life, observes that the city often neglects the importance of aesthetics and the appreciation of the arts.

In addition, security has become a constant concern for Luiz. Violence and crime on the city's streets undermine his sense of peace and tranquility. He finds himself constantly on the alert, looking for ways to protect himself and avoid dangerous situations. This constant concern for his safety affects his well-being and way of life.

Certainly, the monotonous routine and the unchanged urban landscape of São Paulo contribute to Luiz's tiredness. He craves new challenges, an atmosphere that inspires him to explore unknown horizons and discover new perspectives. The daily repetition of the same streets, the same buildings, and the same scenery has become suffocating for his creativity and his search for new stories to tell.

Faced with these challenges, Luiz felt an urgent need to seek new perspectives and motivations for his life. The young writer was still facing a major challenge: creating a new story. He's been trying for weeks to write something new and innovative, but has found it difficult to find inspiration. Mancini is frustrated, doesn't know how to deal with his lack of desire to write, and feels pressured by his friends and family who believe he is wasting his life.

He looks out of the window of his penthouse in Higienópolis and sees the movement of the streets below, but finds nothing to inspire him. The city, which has always been a source of inspiration for him, now seems gray and monotonous. He begins to wonder whether life as a writer is worth living, whether he should move on, or whether it's time for a career change.

Mancini's restlessness begins to affect his personal life and he starts to withdraw from his friends and family. He locked himself in his apartment and refused to go out. His routine became monotonous and dull, and his lack of inspiration only increased...

On a Friday, he felt like he hadn't slept. The writer's mind seemed to be foggy, and he felt extremely tired. He looked at his watch and realized that it was already past 10 a.m. He then thought about how he could make the most of the day, since he hadn't slept well during the night. Then an idea popped into his head: why not go to Paris?

Luiz had visited Paris before, but back then, he wasn't a writer. Now, with a creative block lasting weeks, he felt he needed new inspiration. Paris, the city of lights and art, seemed the perfect place to find what he needed. What's more, July is the most interesting time of year to visit the city, as it's summer in France.

He got out of bed and started packing his suitcase. He put some clothes, his laptop, and some books in his backpack and left the house. The writer decided to take a cab to the airport, as there was a lot of traffic that day.

On the way to the airport, he began to think about everything he could find in Paris. The narrow streets, the charming cafés, the Eiffel Tower, and, above all, the culture and art that permeated the city. He knew he had to find something that would motivate him to write again.

Finally, he arrived at the airport and checked in. He boarded the plane and began to dream of all that Paris had to offer. As the plane crossed the Atlantic Ocean, Luiz closed his eyes and gave himself over to his thoughts. His mind began to fill with vibrant images of Paris. He saw himself walking through the cobbled streets of the Montmartre district, with its street artists and quaint cafés. He imagined himself sitting in one of these cafés, savoring a fresh croissant while watching people go by. Museums also occupied a special place in his daydreams. He found himself in front of the Louvre's masterpieces, such as Leonardo da Vinci's Mona Lisa and the Venus de Milo.

During the flight, the Brazilian felt he was searching for meaning, for a deep connection with himself and the world around him. The capital of France, with its rich history, stunning architecture, and bohemian atmosphere, seemed to be the ideal setting for this search.

As the plane approaches its destination, Luiz opens his eyes and looks out of the window. The clouds are slowly dissipating that late afternoon, revealing a breathtaking view of the city of Paris below. His heart fills with anticipation and determination. He is ready to explore the streets of Paris, the museums, and the experiences that await him.

Already at Paris-Orly Airport, Luiz is waiting for his luggage on the airport conveyor belt, then he notices an elegant woman sitting next to him, also waiting for her bags. Driven by curiosity and the desire to obtain useful

information for his stay in Paris, he decides to strike up a friendly conversation with the woman.

"Sorry to intrude, but I'm planning my stay in Paris and I'd like to know which is the best hotel to stay in," Luiz asked the woman with a friendly smile.

The woman, with an air of sophistication, turned to Luiz and replied:

"Without a doubt, the Hotel Ritz Paris is the best hotel to stay in. However, I must warn you, it is known for being quite expensive."

Luiz listened attentively, reflecting on what the woman had just said. He pondered for a moment and, with a determined expression, replied:

"I understand that the Ritz Paris may have a significantly high price tag, but I believe that the experience is worth more than simply saving up for nothing. I want to make the most of my stay in Paris, experiencing the charm the city has to offer."

The woman smiles, appreciating Luiz's perspective. She agrees and says:

"You're absolutely right. Paris is a unique city, and the experiences you have here can inspire and enrich your life. Don't be afraid to allow yourself to enjoy moments of luxury and enchantment."

Luiz expresses his gratitude to the woman for her words and the valuable information shared. They continue to chat animatedly, immersing themselves in a kind of "exchange" of knowledge about the city.

The woman mentions some of the most renowned restaurants in Paris, such as Le Jules Verne, located on the Eiffel Tower, offering a breathtaking view of the city while enjoying a unique gastronomic experience. She also mentions Le Comptoir du Relais in Saint-Germain-des-Prés, known for its authentic French cuisine and cozy atmosphere.

As for interesting neighborhoods, she suggests Luiz explore Montmartre, with its bohemian atmosphere and the famous Sacré-Cœ ur Basilica. She also highlights the charming neighborhood of Le Marais, with its narrow streets, fashionable stores, and rich cultural history.

As they talk, the woman finds her suitcase at the baggage claim, showing a bit of haste when she sees the time on her watch. She apologizes, explaining that she is late for an important dinner in the city.

"Luiz, it's been a pleasure talking to you and sharing some tips about Paris. I hope you enjoy every moment in this wonderful city. Now I have to rush off to my appointment. I wish you an unforgettable stay and many enriching experiences," she says with a smile.

Luiz thanks the woman again for her generosity in sharing her knowledge and wishes her a great evening. They say goodbye, each going their separate ways in the exciting and enchanting city of Paris.

Mancini spots his suitcase on the luggage belt and hurries to pick it up, feeling a momentary relief at having it in his hands. With his bags in hand, he heads for the airport exit, where there is an area reserved for cabs.

He raises his hand to attract the attention of an available cab. A black sedan car pulls up in front of him. The driver, a nice, well-dressed man, gets out of the vehicle and offers to help Luiz with his bags.

"Good afternoon, sir. Where can I take you?" the driver asks, smiling.

Luiz, with a determined countenance, replies:

"To the Hotel Ritz Paris, please."

The driver nods, opens the trunk, and carefully places Luiz's suitcases in the designated space. He then gets back behind the wheel and adjusts the mirrors before starting the journey.

As the cab drives through the busy streets of Paris, Luiz gazes out of the window at the ever-changing landscape. He observes the different neighborhoods and regions he passes through, each with its own distinct atmosphere and charm.

Leaving Paris-Orly Airport, the cab passes through the town of Arcueil, with its tree-lined streets and charming houses. It then passes through Montrouge and Malakoff, where Luiz catches a glimpse of the daily life of the locals, with their cafés and small shops.

The journey continues through Vanves and Issy-les-Moulineaux, revealing a mix of residential and business buildings. Luiz appreciates the diversity of the urban scenes that pass before his eyes.

As the cab enters the 15th arrondissement of Paris, Luiz is enchanted by the Statue of Liberty Paris, a replica of the Statue of Liberty located on the banks of the River Seine. It's a moment of connection between Paris and New York, a symbol of freedom and inspiration.

Crossing into the 16th arrondissement of Paris, the cab offers a breathtaking view of the Jardin du Trocadéro, with its large green area and a splendid view of the Eiffel Tower in the background. Luiz feels immersed in the grandeur of Paris, with a mixture of emotions ranging from admiration to awe.

As the cab continues on its way, Luiz spots the Musée d'Orsay in the distance, with its impressive architecture and renowned art collection. Although it's not possible to explore it up close at the moment, the mere sight of the museum arouses his curiosity and increases his anticipation of the cultural riches that Paris has to offer.

The walk through the Tuileries Garden enchants Luiz with its tree-lined boulevards, elegant fountains as well as classical sculptures. The tranquil and refined atmosphere provides a pleasant contrast to the bustle of the streets.

Finally, the cab stops in front of the iconic Hotel Ritz Paris. Luiz expresses his gratitude to the driver, who kindly removes his suitcases from the trunk. With a farewell smile, Luiz enters the majestic lobby of the hotel, ready to begin his stay and explore all the charms that Paris has in store for him.

The Parisian atmosphere continues to envelop him, bringing a sense of excitement and renewal as he enters the world of elegance and sophistication of the Hotel Ritz Paris.

As the evening progresses and the city lights begin to twinkle, Luiz arrives at the imposing Hotel Ritz Paris. He is warmly welcomed by one of the hotel staff, who kindly takes his suitcase and escorts him to reception. Luiz can't help but admire the splendor and luxury that surrounds him. The lobby is elegantly decorated, with exquisite furniture, dazzling chandeliers, and details that reflect the hotel's classic charm.

On arriving at the reception, Luiz is greeted by Jules (name written on the receptionist's badge), who greets him with a warm smile. Jules, dressed in an impeccable navy blue uniform, conveys professionalism and courtesy in his service. Luiz immediately feels welcomed and confident that he will have an exceptional stay at the hotel. Jules looks at Mancini and says:

"Good evening, sir. Welcome to the Hotel Ritz Paris. How can I help you? And what is your name?"

Luiz replies:

"Good evening. My name is Luiz. I'd like to stay here for a long time, without a specific check-out date."

The receptionist picked up the hotel's official phone and said:

"I understand, Mr. Luiz. I'll check our system for room availability for an extended stay. Please wait a moment."

Jules calls the accommodation team and, after a few moments, returns with the information requested:

"Mr. Luiz, due to your preference for an extended stay, we only have our Prestige Suites available. They are: Coco Chanel Suite, where Coco Chanel herself lived for 34 years; Vendôme Suite, with ample space and lounge; Mansart Suite, a tribute to the architect Jules Hardouin-Mansart, with a terrace containing a beautiful view of the city of Paris; F. Scott Fitzgerald Suite, extremely spacious. Scott Fitzgerald Suite, extremely spacious and opulent, 1920s style; Marcel Proust Suite, a tribute to the renowned French writer, a regular at the Ritz Paris. Wood paneling gives the feeling of a private library crossed with a bachelor's apartment; and the Opéra Suite, with a perfect view through the theatrical arch windows towards the iconic Opéra Garnier Spacious, majestic and incredibly well-lit, offers the ideal setting for your own drama and story."

Luiz is overwhelmed by the beauty and stories behind each suite. He is torn between the Opéra Suite and the Marcel Proust Suite, enchanted by the elegance and panoramic view offered by the former. In an attempt to decide which suite to stay in, he asks the receptionist:

"Jules, these suites are incredible! I'm in doubt between the Opéra Suite and the Marcel Proust Suite. Could you give me more details about them?"

Jules then turns to Luiz Mancini:

"Certainly, Mr. Luiz. The Opéra Suite offers a perfect view of the Opéra Garnier through the theatrical arched windows. It's spacious, majestic, and incredibly well-lit, providing the ideal setting for your own drama and story. The Marcel Proust Suite, on the other hand, is a living tribute to one of France's greatest writers. With wood paneling reminiscent of a private library, it's an enchanting blend of elegance and comfort."

Luiz ponders for a moment, absorbing the information provided by Jules. Then he makes his choice of the suite:

"I think I'll opt for the Opéra Suite. The beautiful view of the Opéra Garnier and the spacious atmosphere have won me over. It seems perfect for my stay here."

The receptionist replies:

"Excellent choice, Mr. Luiz. I'm sure you'll enjoy a magnificent stay in the Opéra Suite. Allow me to make the necessary arrangements to ensure that everything is ready for your arrival."

In this way, the receptionist at the Hotel Ritz Paris gives Luiz all the information he needs about the Opéra Suite. He explains that the monthly price for the suite is 15,000 euros, offering an ideal option for an extended stay. Alternatively, Luiz has the option of daily rates, which cost approximately 2,500 euros per day.

When considering the options, Luiz realizes that staying in the Opéra Suite for three months would be a unique opportunity to experience Parisian life in a more immersive way. He decides to inform Jules of his decision and tells her that he will pay with his credit card.

Jokingly, Luiz comments that the card bill will certainly give him a "heart attack" due to the many zeros that will appear. However, he says that the experience of living as a mad writer and poet in the City of Light will be worth every penny.

Jules, with a friendly smile, understands Luiz's excitement and agrees that this unique experience will certainly be worth the investment. He assures Luiz that he will take care of all the necessary arrangements to process the payment on the credit card, ensuring that everything is ready for Luiz's stay.

Luiz expresses his gratitude for Jules' attention and care, feeling confident and excited to have chosen the Opéra Suite as his temporary home in Paris. He can't wait to start his new "life" in the City of Light, enjoying all the luxury and comfort offered by the Hotel Ritz Paris.

With the confirmation of Luiz's stay in the Opéra Suite, Jules hands the Brazilian writer his credit card, finalizing the payment process. The receptionist then kindly takes Luiz's suitcases and is ready to take them up to his room.

Luiz, appreciating the grandeur of the hotel hall, with its luxurious and imposing decoration, admires the bars and restaurants located on the first floor of the Ritz Paris. Intrigued by the inviting atmosphere and the promise of an exceptional gastronomic experience, Luiz decides to explore these spaces before heading to his room.

With a smile, Luiz approaches Jules again and makes a request: he would like Jules to leave his bags inside the room while he enjoys the gastronomic options offered by the hotel. He expresses his desire to taste something delicious before retiring to the Opéra Suite to rest.

Jules, always attentive, readily agrees to accommodate Luiz's suitcases in the room, ensuring that everything is organized and safe. He gives Luiz the instructions he needs to find the bars and restaurants, as well as suggesting some of the dishes and drinks featured on the hotel menu.

Luiz thanks Jules for his kindness and guidance, feeling welcome and excited to explore the gastronomic options on offer at the Ritz Paris. With a sense of anticipation and curiosity, he heads toward the bars and restaurants, eager to indulge in the exquisite cuisine that awaits him.

Before indulging in the culinary delights, Luiz decides to take the opportunity to explore the charming reception rooms located on the first floor of the Ritz Paris. Driven by curiosity and the desire to marvel at the beauty of the place, he follows the path indicated by Jules and explores the hotel's elegant and luxurious rooms.

The first room Luiz visits is the iconic Salon d'Été (summer salon). As he enters, his eyes light up with the optimistic and radiant atmosphere that surrounds the room, regardless of the weather conditions outside. The lounge is bathed in natural light, with large windows offering a breathtaking view of the hotel's landscaped Grand Jardin.

On sunny days, the Salon d'Été opens onto the terrace, allowing guests to enjoy the cool breeze and enchanting scenery. The connection with nature is a striking feature of this room, and the large windows and glass atrium ensure that the beauty of the outside is brought inside, creating a sense of harmony and tranquility.

The ambiance of the Salon d'Été is spacious and bright, with decor carefully selected to evoke the vibrant and cheerful atmosphere of summer. The predominant coloring is light and white, creating a feeling of freshness and lightness. The green armchairs add a touch of color and elegance to the space, providing comfort and a welcoming place for guests to relax.

In addition, Luiz notes that the Salon d'Été is versatile and can be adapted to meet the needs of different events. The writer sees in Jules' guide that on some occasions, it can be combined with the Psyché and Louis XV salons, creating one continuous space or three adjoining spaces, thus making it possible to accommodate a larger number of people or offer different settings for different activities.

As Mancini explores the Salon d'Été, he is enchanted by the breathtaking view of the Ritz Paris garden. The sense of peace and serenity that permeates the environment invites him to enjoy a moment of contemplation, where he can appreciate the lush nature around him.

With the starry sky illuminating the night, Luiz decides to explore the majestic Grand Jardin of the Hotel Ritz Paris. As he approaches, he spots

some guests sitting at outdoor tables, engaged in animated conversation, while enjoying their drinks and cigarettes. The garden is beautifully lit, creating a magical and inviting atmosphere.

Upon entering the Grand Jardin, Luiz feels immersed in a truly private oasis in the heart of the city. His eyes are drawn to the bunches of white flowers and magnolias that adorn the room, spreading a soft, enchanting fragrance. The garden reveals private alcoves, hidden between hedges, providing intimate and welcoming spaces for guests to enjoy moments of tranquility and contemplation.

Luiz decides to take advantage of the magic of the Grand Jardin and finds a spot on the grass to sit down. He lets himself be enveloped by the lush greenery of the place, breathing deeply to absorb the serenity and invigorating energy emanating from the garden. Looking up, he contemplates the starry sky and the bright moon, feeling connected to nature and the grandeur of the universe.

The Grand Jardin at the Ritz Paris is truly unique in its beauty and charm. In addition to its vast expanse, the garden is romantic and timeless, captivating the senses of those who visit it. The presence of a water fountain adds a touch of serenity and provides a soft ambient sound, creating a relaxing and inspiring atmosphere.

Luiz lets himself be carried away by the enchanting atmosphere of the Grand Jardin, knowing that this special space will be a haven during his stay at the Ritz Paris. He appreciates the opportunity to enjoy such a peaceful and welcoming environment, where he can escape the hustle and bustle of the city and connect with the natural beauty around him.

Sitting on the grass in the garden, Luiz reflects on how lucky he is to be able to experience such memorable moments in such a unique place. He recognizes that the Grand Jardin is a treasure in the heart of Paris, offering guests an exceptional and unique experience.With the gentle breeze caressing his face and the sight of the garden illuminated by starlight, Luiz surrenders to a moment of peace and gratitude.

Luiz then leaves the charming Grand Jardin and heads for the Salon Psyché, curious to explore the surroundings and witness the unique atmosphere of the place. However, he realizes that there is a meeting in progress, with a select group of guests enjoying the event. Even though he can't enter, Luiz doesn't miss the opportunity to admire the beauty and striking features of the salon.

Salon Psyché exudes an aura of warmth and elegance that perfectly reflects the meaning of its name. Looking at it from the outside, Luiz is impressed by the grandeur of the salon and its historical importance, since it is considered a Historic Monument. This distinction gives the room an air of special occasion, transporting visitors to an atmosphere of refinement and sophistication.

Luiz is amazed by the carefully crafted details in the salon. The Aubusson tapestry, with its intricate designs and rich colors, is a true masterpiece that lends an artistic touch to the space. Each meticulously woven thread tells a story, adding even more charm and beauty to the room.

In addition, Luiz notices the meticulously carved woodwork that adorns the room. The delicate shapes and ornate details reveal the craftsmanship behind these pieces, adding a touch of classic elegance to the room.

Curious to learn more about the historical heritage of the Ritz Paris, Luiz makes his way to the elegant Salon Vendôme. This room exudes opulence and sophistication, with its sparkling chandeliers, exquisite furniture, and carefully arranged works of art. Luiz feels like a privileged guest, immersed in an atmosphere of refinement and good taste.

Luiz continues his exploration of the Hotel Ritz Paris and heads for the Louis XV Salon. This magnificent salon was named after King Louis XV, known for his majesty and popularity. Upon entering, Luiz is enchanted by the spectacular gilded woodwork, the long mirrors that enlarge the space, and the dazzling crystal chandeliers. Every detail of the hall emanates an air of refinement and elegance reminiscent of the grandeur of the time.

After briefly appreciating the beauty of the Salon Louis XV, Luiz feels the need to satisfy his hunger and quickly heads to the Salon de Gramont. This room, whose elegant decor reflects its noble name, offers an atmosphere of calm and absolute privacy. Two separate entrances, one of which leads to the enchanting Grand Jardin, give the space a feeling of tranquility and serenity.

Luiz notices the reference to the Duke of Gramont, famous at Versailles, and imagines the moments of conviviality and relaxation that this room has witnessed over the years. With its exquisite décor and serene atmosphere, the Salon de Gramont provides a cozy refuge for guests, where they can enjoy moments of privacy and relaxation.

Although his visit to the Salon de Gramont is brief, Luiz retains the feeling of tranquility and sophistication that the environment conveys. He continues on his way, aware that there is still much to discover and experience at the Hotel Ritz Paris.

Then Luiz, already wanting something to eat, checks the time on his watch and realizes that it's already 10:23 p.m. He decides to hurry to Bar Vendôme for dinner. When he arrives, he is greeted by the elegant and captivating atmosphere of the Parisian brasserie. The red velvet stools, the impeccable service, and the lively, relaxed atmosphere create a unique experience. The menu offers a variety of options, catering to all tastes and desires. From the first coffee to the last drink, Bar Vendôme's famous Belle Époque glass roof embodies the welcoming essence of the Ritz Paris.

The writer notices that the bar is quite busy, but with a keen eye, he manages to find an empty table where he can settle down comfortably. He examines the menu and, directing his interest to the main courses, comes across some delicious options. The Linguine, prepared with roasted prawns, lobster bisque, garlic, and chili peppers, awakens his taste buds with an explosion of flavors.

Another option that catches his eyes is the Fresh French Sole Fish, accompanied by a creamy ballotine and fennel confit, spiced with redcurrant and fennel sauce. The detailed description of the dishes sparks your imagination and transports you on a gastronomic journey in which you can savor every element with pleasure.

The Bouillabaisse de Salmonete, cooked à la plancha, with confit potatoes, mussels in escabeche, and a saffron rockfish soup, also catches your eye. The combination of fresh flavors and the delicacy of the fish promise a unique and memorable experience.

While Mancini ponders his choices, he also comes across meat options, such as the fried fillet "aux pâturages", accompanied by dauphine potatoes, shallot compote, and a green pepper sauce with cognac. The veal, prepared with roast cutlet, artichoke mousseline and artichoke barigoule, and meat juice, also stands out as a tempting option.

Finally, the French Chicken from Cyril Deglutire's farm in Bresse, roasted supreme and accompanied by confit leg calamari pasta, smoked corn, pistachios, and a Matifoc dry rancio wine sauce, piques Luiz's interest with its balance of flavors and refined ingredients.

With so many delicious options at his disposal, Luiz chooses his main course carefully. He then raises his hand to call the waiter. With a welcoming smile, the waiter approaches the table and eagerly awaits Luiz's order. With confidence, Luiz declares his choice: Linguine with roasted prawns, lobster bisque, garlic, and chili peppers.

The waiter, attentive to detail, carefully notes down Luiz's order in his notepad and asks him to confirm if he would like any starters before the main course. However, Luiz politely refuses, stating that he is only looking forward to the main course. He adds that he would like to accompany his meal with a refreshing lemon soda.

With his order taken, the waiter moves away from the table and heads for the kitchen, where the chefs at the Ritz Paris are hard at work preparing each dish with masterly precision. Luiz waits patiently, immersed in the lively and elegant atmosphere of Bar Vendôme, eager to taste the irresistible flavors that will soon arrive at his table.

While he waits for his main course, Luiz enjoys the sophisticated atmosphere and observes the movement around him. The lively conversations, the clinking glasses, and the soft music that fills the air create a harmonious symphony of pleasant moments. The writer's ears were captivated by the soft sound of the piano, accompanied by the sweet sound of the violin. Curious, he looked for the source of the music and soon spotted two talented musicians positioned to his right, who enchanted everyone with their performance.

The melody that filled the air was Franz Schubert's "Ständchen", a classical composition that seemed to fit in perfectly with the refined atmosphere of the bar. Luiz felt enveloped by the music, letting himself be carried away by the melodious notes that danced in the air. It was as if the harmony of the music perfectly matched the sophisticated atmosphere of the place.

While he was enjoying the music, Luiz saw the waiter approaching with his lemon soda. He thanked the waiter with a smile, grateful for his attention. The waiter kindly asked if he was enjoying the music and offered to change the song if necessary. However, Luiz promptly replied that there was no need to make any changes, as he thought the sound was perfect for the moment.

Mancini enjoyed every sip of the lemon soda, letting the invigorating citrus flavor quench his thirst. The music continued to fill the room, and he let himself be enveloped by the sophisticated and inspiring atmosphere of Bar Vendôme. Every chord and note seemed to blend harmoniously with the surroundings, creating a very interesting sensory experience. While the wait for the main course continued, Luiz enjoyed the present moment, letting himself be carried away by the music and the enchanting atmosphere around him.

The Linguine arrived at Luiz's table, and he couldn't resist the first bite. The taste of the dish is simply divine. The pasta is perfectly cooked, with a soft

and delicate texture. The roasted prawns are juicy and full of flavor, combining harmoniously with the rich lobster bisque. The sauce, with garlic and chili peppers, adds a hint of spiciness that elevates the dish to an exceptional level of flavor.

Every bite is an explosion of flavors on your palate, and Luiz savors every bite with pleasure. The combination of ingredients creates a symphony of taste, where each element complements each other perfectly. He feels grateful for having chosen this dish, which has now become an unforgettable gastronomic experience.

After finishing his meal, Luiz decides to go up the elegant stairs of the Ritz Paris to his room. He takes his cell phone out of his pocket and looks up the floor and suite number that will be his new home for the next few months. With a smile on his face, he marvels at the hotel's decor as he climbs the top floors.

With every step he takes, Luiz admires the luxurious carpet beneath his feet, the exquisite details on the walls, and the sparkle of the chandeliers. The atmosphere is a true work of art, a reflection of the glamor and sophistication of the Ritz Paris.

Walking in the City of Light

Finally, he arrives at the door of the Suite, his private refuge. When he opens the door, he is greeted by an imposing space, elegantly decorated and full of comfort. Luiz feels welcomed and can call this place his new home for a long time.

He looks around, appreciating every detail of the suite. From the elegant furniture to the theatrical arched windows overlooking the iconic Opéra Garnier and the city of Paris, everything has been carefully selected to provide a glamorous stay.

The writer gazes at the breathtaking view from the window, amazed at how Paris comes alive at night. The city shines brightly, as if each light were a star illuminating the night sky. He understands why Paris is known as the City of Light, as the enveloping, magical atmosphere of the city reveals itself before his eyes.

Determined to rest after a day full of emotions, Luiz takes off his clothes and heads for the bathroom. The hot water of the shower envelops his body, relaxing his tired muscles. Every drop that falls on his skin is like a balm, relieving the accumulated fatigue of the day and preparing him for a deep rest.

After his shower, Luiz returns to his room and walks towards the bed. The softness of the mattress invites him to lie down, and he surrenders to the coziness of the pure linen sheet. His body craves a well-deserved rest, and his eyes begin to close gently. The exhaustion of the last few days envelops him, and he lets himself be carried away by the comfort of the moment. The silence of the room and the tranquility of the surroundings calm his agitated mind, allowing him to surrender to the arms of sleep. Each breath becomes more serene and deeper, as he drifts off into the world of dreams...

The next day, Mancini wakes up, awakened by the rays of sunlight that gently invade his room, illuminating every corner. He gets out of bed, feeling refreshed after a restful night's sleep. As he stretches, his ear catches the insistent sound of the telephone next to him. He promptly picks it up and is greeted by the hotel concierge, Paul.

The concierge, with his polite voice, offers him the option of taking breakfast up to Luiz's suite or going downstairs to enjoy it at the Bar Vendôme. Luiz smiles in appreciation and decides that today he wants to enjoy his coffee in the lively and elegant atmosphere of the bar. However, he informs Paul that for the next few days, he would prefer to enjoy breakfast in his suite, enjoying the privacy and comfort of the space.

After his conversation with Paul, Luiz dresses elegantly, carefully choosing each piece of his outfit. He walks down the hotel's imposing staircase, appreciating the grandeur of his surroundings. With every step, he feels enveloped by the sophisticated and vibrant atmosphere of the Ritz Paris.

Arriving at the Bar Vendôme, Luiz chooses a strategically positioned table, allowing him to enjoy his surroundings. While sipping his coffee, he notices a stunning woman watching him discreetly. Her blonde hair shines in the soft light and her blue eyes capture his attention like glittering sapphires.

Luiz stares at the woman with a mixture of admiration and fascination. There is something about her sapphire-blue eyes that captivates him deeply. It's as if they've known each other for a long time as if there's an inexplicable connection between them. The mysterious aura surrounding the woman only adds to the magnetism she exudes.

So much so that he feels a magnetic attraction, an energy that pulls him towards her. Every glance, every gesture, every smile thrown in his direction seems to penetrate his soul, awakening intense and unknown emotions. He feels hypnotized by her presence as if he were in a state of enchantment.

However, despite feeling a deep connection, Luiz doesn't find the courage to approach her. A mixture of fear and uncertainty prevents him from taking the next step. He wonders if she feels the same magnetism if she is also captured by the intensity of the moment.

That fleeting encounter at the Bar Vendôme awakens a flame inside Luiz, a flame that warms his heart and makes him wonder what could happen if they allowed themselves to get to know each other better. His curiosity and desire to uncover the secrets behind that deep, penetrating gaze grow with every second.

Luiz feels a mixture of conflicting emotions - attraction and insecurity intertwine in his mind and heart. He wonders whether he should take a risk, whether he should get closer and unravel the mysteries surrounding this enigmatic woman. The desire to know more, to explore what could arise from this unexpected connection, fights against the fears and shyness that consume him.

While the woman remains in his field of vision, Luiz loses himself in thought and reflection. He knows that this fleeting encounter could turn into something special, a unique and memorable story. The intensity of the moment inspires him to face his fears, to allow himself to dive into that possible love story.

However, for the time being, he just cherishes the image of the woman in his mind, keeping that deep, attractive gaze as a precious memory. Luiz feels that this encounter marked the beginning of something special, something that could transform his life in unimaginable ways.

Mancini takes one last look at the mysterious woman at the Bar Vendôme, feeling an inexplicable connection, but decides to let fate decide the course of this story. He leaves the Ritz hotel with a desire to get to know Paris.

On leaving the hotel, he finds himself in an enchanting square, dominated by the imposing Vendôme Column, an iconic monument celebrating the conquests of Napoleon Bonaparte. The column, with its ornate details and majestic statue at the top, conveys a sense of historical grandeur.

While looking at the column, Luiz comes across an intriguing sight: the old and prestigious Louis Vuitton store. The elegant and classic façade attracts a crowd of admirers, all eager to enter and explore the brand's luxurious products. He notices the long queue stretching down the sidewalk, proof of the store's popularity and exclusivity.

Afterward, the writer takes his cell phone out of his pocket, ready to plan his day in Paris. He knows that the city is full of historical, cultural, and artistic wonders waiting to be discovered. Consulting his travel guide and maps, he begins to ponder the places he wants to explore. He sees that he is located between the 8th Arrondissement of Paris and the 2nd Arrondissement of Paris.

So, Mancini decides to explore the 2nd arrondissement of Paris, he begins his journey in this charming neighborhood. The 2nd arrondissement, also known as the Bourse, maybe the smallest of Paris' 20 districts, but it hides a world of wonders that many tourist guides fail to mention. With its small size, it offers a multitude of interesting attractions to see and do.

The writer begins his tour with the famous Parisian-covered passages, known as "passages couverts". These passages came into being at the end of the 18th century, after the French Revolution, when many properties previously belonging to religious orders and the Catholic Church were sold off and nationalized. The developers who acquired these properties saw an opportunity to maximize their profits by dividing them into passages lined with small businesses and boutiques.

At that time, Paris still retained much of its medieval character, and shopping was a challenging task. You had to brave narrow, muddy streets, wade through crowds, dodge horses, and endure the stench that permeated the city. Covered passageways emerged as an innovative solution, transforming the Parisian shopping scene. With their glass ceilings letting in sunlight, tiled floors keeping feet dry and a plethora of stores and cafés lined up, they became not only commercial spaces but also meeting places for the Parisian elite.

In the 2nd arrondissement, you'll find the highest concentration of these covered passages, of which there are less than 30 left in the city. Each one has its own identity and unique characteristics, making for a fascinating experience. It's like entering a hidden world of Paris, where you can appreciate the detailed architecture while indulging in shopping, dining, and social interaction.

In order to get to know the passages and galleries, Luiz decides to visit nine covered passages and historic galleries, starting his journey at Galerie Vivienne, considered the most elegant arcade in the 2nd arrondissement.

At the luxurious Galerie Vivienne, with entrances at 6 Rue Vivienne, 5 Rue de la Banque, and Rue des Petits-Champs, Luiz is enchanted by the original mosaic floors from 1823, carefully restored. The steel and glass roof rises above a rotunda, providing a charming setting in which to explore the many high-end stores, gift boutiques, and specialty establishments. The antique and vintage stores attract the attention of many aficionados.

During his stroll through the gallery, Luiz decides to make a stop at Legrand Filles et Fils, known for its excellent selection of wines and gourmet food. He contemplates taking part in a special wine-tasting event or enjoying a meal at the adjacent restaurant, Le Comptoir de Dégustation. On the other side of the passageway, Bistrot Vivienne offers French culinary favorites.

While exploring Galerie Vivienne, Luiz can't resist the temptation to taste some typical French wines. He enjoys Saint-Émilion, a robust and elegant red wine, known for its great aging potential and balanced, concentrated flavors. He then enjoys a Chablis, a renowned white wine from the Burgundy region, which has a high concentration of minerality, hints of honey, and a remarkable complexity. Luiz also tries a Sancerre, produced in the vineyards of the Loire Valley, which offers a fresh and balanced taste with unique minerality characteristics. Finally, he enjoys a Rosé de Provence wine, produced in the Provence region, known for its delicate, floral, and aromatic rosés.

Impressed by the quality and affordability of French wines, Luiz decides to buy a bottle of Chablis white wine to enjoy during his exploration of the neighborhood.

He appreciates the opportunity to taste these wine gems while indulging in the cultural and architectural discoveries of the 2nd arrondissement of Paris. It's a unique experience where he can appreciate the richness of French food and wine, a luxury that is not always accessible in his home country.

Luiz, now with his bottle of Chablis in hand, continues his journey through the 2nd arrondissement of Paris. He then decided to explore the Passage Choiseul, a charming space featuring Korean, Japanese, and other Asian boutiques and bistros. That afternoon, the passage was unusually empty, giving Luiz the opportunity to enjoy the quiet and charming atmosphere.

This passage, dating from 1827, is an extension of the Rue de Choiseul and has a variety of stores, galleries, and boutiques, including Korean, Japanese, and other Asian businesses. This Asian influence in the area dates back to *the 1970s, when Japanese fashion designer Kenzo Takada opened his first boutique in Paris on Passage Choiseul, creating a buzz in the area and attracting Japanese tourists. Since then, the Asian presence and influence in the area have continued to grow.*

While strolling along Passage Choiseul, Luiz takes the opportunity to try a delicious temaki from one of the local restaurants, immersing himself in the flavors and culture of Asian cuisine. After this experience, he heads towards the Passage des Princes, an arcade in the 2nd district dedicated to toys and games.

Built-in 1860, the Passage des Princes is notable for being the last covered arcade authorized during the time of Baron Haussmann, who made several changes to the city. Although it was destroyed in 1885, it was rebuilt in 1995 by two architects, retaining most of its original features. The passage features a beautiful stained glass dome and two galleries covered with high steel and glass roofs, forming a right angle with charming arabesques.

The highlight of the Passage des Princes is its unique theme, which is highly popular with children and teenagers: all the stores specialize in toys, models, and games of all kinds, including video games. It's a veritable paradise for lovers of fun and entertainment. Luiz enters the passageway, amazed by the new and enchanting atmosphere that surrounds him. He observes the shop windows full of fascinating toys, and the enthusiasm of the children and young people exploring the diversity of games available.

As he leaves the Passage des Princes, Luiz reflects on the cultural and historical wealth he has found in the 2nd district of Paris. These covered passages, as well as offering a refuge from the weather and a charming setting for shopping and strolling, preserve a piece of the past and enrich the visitor experience

Luiz continues his exploration of the charms of the 2nd arrondissement of Paris, now heading for the Passage des Panoramas. This passage opened in 1800 and is famous for being one of the first public spaces in the city to be lit by gas, has a rich history, and is a true paradise for stamp and coin collectors.

The Passage des Panoramas forms an enchanting labyrinth, connecting to several other glass-roofed galleries, such as the Galerie Saint-Marc, Galerie Feydeau, Galerie Montmartre, and Galerie des Variétés. Located within a large block surrounded by emblematic Paris streets such as Boulevard Montmartre, Rue Montmartre, Rue Saint-Marc, and Rue Vivienne, this passage is an invitation to explore its corridors and discover the gems it holds.

As he enters the Passage des Panoramas, he finds a nostalgic atmosphere full of history. Dealers specializing in antiques, stamps, and old coins occupy many of the stores, keeping the tradition of this space alive since its inauguration. However, over the years, the passage has also welcomed art galleries, wine stores, clothing boutiques, and charming cafés and bistros, making it even more diverse and attractive.

Luiz, who is passionate about collecting memorabilia, can't resist buying an old 5 Franc coin from 1971. He is enchanted by the beautiful olive leaf design on the coin, and the sentimental value it carries will be a special souvenir of his visit to the Passage des Panoramas.

As he wanders through the galleries and stores of this passage, Mancini immerses himself in the vintage atmosphere and allows himself to get lost in the labyrinth of charms that stretches out before his eyes. Parts of the passage may show signs of wear and tear, adding even more charm and authenticity to the place. Other areas are constantly being rebuilt, bringing a sense of renewal and evolution to the space.

Luiz is amazed by the variety of stores and boutiques near the entrances to the passage. He decides to explore Rue Vivienne further, a charming street which, as he heads south for a few blocks, will take him back to Galerie Vivienne, where he begins his journey through the 2nd district.

The writer now heads for the Passage du Grand Cerf. This magnificent arcade, with its three-story glass roof, provides a stunning backdrop to a variety of art stores and boutiques that line its long corridor, with a tiled floor that shimmers under the natural light that penetrates through the steel and glass roof.

The Passage du Grand Cerf is a true paradise for lovers of vintage treasures, art, crafts and unique jewelry. As Luiz walks down the corridor, he comes across a plethora of stores offering an eclectic variety of contents, making the experience of exploring this arcade truly captivating.

As he enters the Passage du Grand Cerf, Luiz marvels at the light that bathes the space, highlighting every detail of the objects on display in the windows. He surrenders to his curiosity and explores each store, enchanted by the carefully selected pieces of art, crafts, and handmade jewelry. The writer *feels as if he is in a parallel universe, where creativity and talent meet in perfect harmony.*

Through the stores of the Passage du Grand Cerf, Luiz has the opportunity to discover real gems, objects that carry unique stories and meanings. He is enchanted by the variety of options available, from vintage decorative pieces to contemporary jewelry, each displaying a special touch of art and craftsmanship.

The Passage du Grand Cerf is accessed via the streets Rue Dussoubs and Rue Saint-Martin, which lead Luiz to this hidden gem in the 2nd district of Paris.

Luiz's next destination is the iconic Passage du Caire, considered to be the oldest arcade in Paris. Despite having a certain appearance of poverty and decay, this historic passage still manages to emanate an aura of its former grandeur, especially when observed from the point where its three walkways converge, allowing sunlight to fall on its pointed glass roof.

Inaugurated in 1798, the Passage du Caire coincided with the fervent Parisian craze for everything related to Egypt, driven by Napoleon's campaign in the country. Looking at the side of the building that houses the main entrance to the passage, you can't help but notice three sculptural images of the Egyptian goddess Hathor, peering curiously at their surroundings.

In addition to its title as the oldest covered gallery in the city, the Passage du Caire boasts other peculiar titles. It is also the longest and narrowest covered passageway in Paris and, perhaps even more uniquely, it is the only one that currently houses wholesale fabric, finishing, and ready-to-wear companies. It's as if there were a microcosm of the clothing industry in Sentier, offering an authentic portrait of an era and a specific segment of the trade.

Despite its unique characteristics, the Passage du Caire does not go unnoticed by the urban transformations taking place around it. Gentrification, which has spread to many areas of Paris, could one day change the landscape of this fascinating place. But for now, this historic passageway remains a captivating and intriguing place to stroll through, allowing visitors to witness all the activity and energy that pulses through its corridors.

Luiz continues his journey to explore the next stop, the majestic Galerie Colbert.

As Mancini enters the gallery, two surprising features catch his eye: firstly, the spectacular rotunda that rises majestically, crowned by a dazzling glass dome. It's an impressive piece of architecture that seems to transport visitors to another era. Secondly, he notices something peculiar about the Galerie Colbert: it houses no commercial stores, apart from a renowned restaurant, Le Grand Colbert, a splendid brasserie that is extremely popular with the locals. The reason behind this commercial absence is clear: the National Library of France acquired the gallery in 1826 and over the decades it has been used to house the prestigious National Institute of Art History and various other cultural institutions.

Although the gallery no longer serves as a shopping and commercial space, it is still possible to visit it. Luiz is thrilled to know that he can walk through this majestic ornate passageway, even if he has to pass through a security checkpoint first. The experience of walking under the glass dome and appreciating the carefully detailed architecture is worth it, especially on a sunny day when the sunlight penetrates through the stained glass windows, creating a spectacle of colors and shadows.

Located between the rues des Petits-Champs and Vivienne, the Galerie Colbert is an architectural gem of Paris that preserves its history and enchants visitors with its timeless beauty. It's one of those gems that, although it can't be explored in its entirety as it once was, still manages to offer a memorable and unique experience to those who venture through its corridors.

And finally, Mancini heads to his last stop, the charming Passage du Bourg l'Abbé. Built-in 1828 by the talented architect Auguste Lusson, it stretches between the Passage du Grand-Cerf and the Passage de l'Ancre - a passageway that still exists and is full of stores, but without the charm of a covered roof.

In the past, the Passage du Bourg l'Abbé connected directly with a street of the same name - not to be confused with the current Rue du Bourg l'Abbé, which was created later. This magnificent passageway, which once displayed all the splendor of its grandeur, competed with and mirrored another, older passageway, the Passage de Saucede, which unfortunately disappeared when the rue de Turbigo was opened in 1854.

Over time, the Passage Le Bourg-l'Abbé has undergone some modifications, such as the reduction of its length during the construction of the Boulevard Sebastopol in 1854 and the creation of the Rue de Palestro. Even with these changes, the entrance to the passage, designed by the talented architect Henri Blondel, remains a true work of art, enriched by the two caryatids sculpted by Aimé Millet, which symbolize commerce and industry.

Today, however, we find the Passage du Bourg l'Abbé in a rather melancholy state. Located in a popular area and undergoing numerous changes over the years, the passage is now undergoing a restoration process to restore it to its former glory and splendor. Even with modest proportions, it has always maintained a certain prestige, but for some reason, the atmosphere around it seems rather sad and sleepy.

Eyes that Steal the Heart

Luiz looks at his watch and realizes that it's already 18:00. The sun is still shining in the city and he decides to enjoy the evening in a nearby park, Square Louvois. This charming green space offers a peaceful refuge in a city known for its numerous public parks and green areas.

Located in the 2nd arrondissement, Square Louvois was created in 1836 on Rue Richelieu, where a theater used to be situated - the first in Paris to provide seating for its spectators. It's a little oasis that wins visitors over with its serene and welcoming atmosphere.

In the center of the square stands the imposing Fontaine Louvois, installed in 1844. This beautiful fountain is adorned with statues created by the sculptor Jean-Baptiste-Jules Klagmann, representing the four main rivers of France: the Seine, the Saône, the Loire, and the Garonne. It is a highlight that attracts the eye and enchants visitors with its timeless beauty.

Around the fountain, benches strategically positioned in a gravel circle invite workers from the nearby offices to come and have lunch there, as well as locals who take advantage of the spot to enjoy the sun and relax. Luiz, still holding his bottle of white Chablis, observes the many people sitting in the park, having pleasant picnics and enjoying the lovely weather.

Feeling a little tired after exploring the galleries and passageways of the 2nd arrondissement of Paris, the writer decides to find a quiet spot on the grass to rest for a while. Sitting in a comfortable spot, he appreciates the serene atmosphere of the park, feeling in harmony with the nature around him. As the sun gradually sets, golden light illuminates the room, creating an aura of calm and serenity.

Luiz decides to open the bottle of white wine and savor its contents, enjoying the delicate aromas and fresh notes that harmonize perfectly with the bucolic setting of the park. While savoring each sip, he admires the people around him, observing their interactions, laughter, and shared joy. It's a moment of tranquillity and contemplation, allowing him to disconnect from the fast pace of the city and immerse himself in the peace offered by Square Louvois.

While Luiz was enjoying his moment of rest in Square Louvois, appreciating the calm and serenity of the park, his eyes were caught by a figure that stood out among the rest. A woman stares at Luiz from afar, engaged in animated conversation with her friends. She is simply stunning, with her light brown hair that shimmers softly in the evening light, and her eyes that display a mesmerizing mix of green and blue, like rare jewels reflecting the sunlight.

She is elegantly dressed, wearing a black shirt with a semi-satin fabric that highlights the beauty of her skin, combined with black pants that fit her body perfectly, highlighting her curves. To complete the look, she wears black high heels that further accentuate her imposing posture. Luiz can't help but admire the beauty and charm of this woman who seems to have stepped straight out of a scene of sophistication and elegance.

Luiz assumes that she may have just left work, given the professional and elegant look she is sporting. As he stares at her, a feeling of fascination takes hold of his heart. Their gazes meet briefly and, as if driven by a desire to get to know this enigmatic woman, Luiz nods to her, lifting his bottle of white Chablis slightly in greeting.

To his surprise and satisfaction, the woman returned the nod and gracefully said goodbye to her friends or colleagues, taking determined steps toward the writer. His heart pounds with anticipation as he anxiously awaits the arrival of the woman who seems to have been made to shine in the crowd.

As she approaches, Luiz can't help but smile shyly and charmingly. Her steps are firm and confident, and the sound of her heels echoes through the park, creating a kind of magical soundtrack that accompanies the unfolding scene.

The woman, Camille, approaches Luiz and sits down next to him, continuing the friendly nod they shared moments before. She turns to him, noticing the bottle of Chablis still in his hands, and with a charming smile, starts the conversation:

"Chablis wine is very good, but I have a thing for red wine," she says, as her eyes sparkle with enthusiasm.

Luiz responds with a certain lightness in his voice, enjoying the moment of connection between them:

"Well, I see. Chablis is lighter, but it's delicious in its way. I like to enjoy it, especially on sunny days like today."

Curious, Luiz decides to ask her name, considering they share a taste for wine:

"And you, red wine lover, what's your name?"

Camille laughs softly, gently introducing herself:

"My name is Camille. It's a pleasure to meet you."

Luiz smiles back, enjoying Camille's presence:

"I'm Luiz, a writer from Brazil. I decided to come to the City of Lights to find inspiration, and new ideas and rediscover this beautiful city."

Curious about Luiz's presence in the city, Camille asks with genuine interest:

"From Brazil? How interesting! And what brought you to Paris? I'm sure this charming city has a lot to offer a talented writer like you."

Luiz thanks her for the compliment and replies sincerely:

"Paris is a place full of history and culture, the perfect environment to stimulate my creativity. I came here to be inspired and to bring new stories to life."

Intrigued, Camille tells Luiz about her work, and ends up explaining why she came to him:

"I work in marketing and I was watching you here in the park, with that curious look on your face, and I found you interesting... You seemed to be surrounded by mysteries and enjoying the moment, and that made me curious to find out more about you." Camille said, with a little laugh.

Luiz is flattered by Camille's interest and thanks her for her friendly approach:

"Well, I'm glad you came to talk to me. It's always nice to meet new people and exchange ideas in a place as beautiful as this."

Camille's curiosity about Luiz's presence in the park is inevitable, and she asks with an intrigued air:

"What brought you here to the park?"

Luiz, with a friendly smile, replies:

"I was exploring the passageways and galleries of the 2nd arrondissement of Paris and decided to come and have a little rest here. The city is so charming and full of fascinating places to visit."

After speaking, Luiz brings the bottle of wine to his lips again and takes a refreshing sip. At that moment, in a surprising and captivating way, Camille takes the bottle from his hand and drinks the wine too. The connection between them seemed to intensify at that moment.

"I hope you don't mind," says Camille with a playful smile. "Wine is simply irresistible at this time of day."

Luiz, impressed by Camille's boldness and friendliness, replies gently:

"Of course, I don't mind. After all, sharing a good wine in good company is always a great idea."

Grateful for the gesture, Camille shows her appreciation:

"Thank you for the sip of wine. Sometimes life reserves unexpected and delightful encounters for us."

With a curious look on his face, Luiz asks intrigued:

"So, what's this interesting place you think I should visit?"

Looking mysterious, Camille gets up from her seat and replies with a captivating smile:

"Ah, you'll have to go with me to find out. It's a special place here in the 2nd arrondissement, I'm sure you'll love it."

Mancini, intrigued by the proposal, gets up too and says:

"Well, in that case, I can't refuse such an intriguing invitation. I'm ready to explore this place with you."

Luiz follows Camille's graceful footsteps through the streets of Paris, being led by her to an enchanting venue: the Comic Opera at the Salle Favart. As they approach the theater, Camille enthusiastically shares information about the Opéra-Comique opera company, which dates back to 1714, becoming a cultural tradition with deep roots in the city:

"Although the Opéra National de Paris is the most famous, the Opéra-Comique is just as remarkable and regularly performs here in the Salle Favart in the 2nd arrondissement," explains Camille, pointing out the magnificent building.

Mancini looks at the theater, amazed at its beauty and elegance. And he says to her:

"Indeed, it's a stunning place. I like opera, but I haven't had the chance to see a performance in Paris yet."

With a smile, Camille shares more about the performances at the Comic Opera:

"The performances here are excellent and the variety of operas is vast. They not only perform the classics, but also new contemporary operas."

Curious, Luiz asks:

"But what exactly does 'comic opera' mean?"

Camille explains amusingly:

"In 19th century France, 'comic opera' wasn't necessarily comic, but rather a lighter musical genre with engaging and exciting stories. It's an enchanting experience for lovers of music and the arts."

Delighted by Camille's suggestion, Luiz replies:

"That sounds fascinating. I'd love to see a comic opera here at the Comic Opera. Thank you for your recommendation."

Camille looks him in the eye and says:

"I'm glad you're excited to see the opera. I'm sure it will be an unforgettable evening."

As they chat, Luiz's curiosity about French culture and the arts grows, and he feels grateful to have found someone like Camille to guide him through this enchanting world.

The Brazilian writer and the French comic opera lover share laughs and stories as they walk towards the theater door.

Upon arriving at the theater, Luiz and Camille come across a billboard with several plays available. Camille, with her knowledge of French culture, suggests that they watch "Cyrano de Bergerac" by Edmond Rostand, a classic and iconic play that is part of France's rich theatrical heritage. Luiz agrees enthusiastically, excited to experience one of the most celebrated works of French literature.

Determined to see the play, they head to the box office and buy tickets for the show that will start at 20:00. With time to spare until the performance begins, they choose to sit at a nearby counter to enjoy the wait.

As they settle down, Luiz asks for some water to refresh himself, while Camille chooses some food to go with the coffee she wants. The atmosphere is pleasant and relaxed, and they take advantage of this moment to talk more about Parisian culture and their life experiences.

Camille, with her contagious enthusiasm, shares stories about the Salle Favart theater and her own experiences of past performances. Luiz listens attentively, captivated by every detail and the passion she transmits when talking about the theater and its plays.

Coffee arrives at the table, filling the room with a cozy aroma. Luiz and Camille share smiles as they toast to that special moment in Paris, in each other's company.

As the time for the play approaches, they feel their excitement grow. The evening light begins to give way to the enchanting illumination of the theater, creating a magical and mysterious atmosphere.

Finally, the long-awaited hour arrives. They make their way to the performance hall, finding their seats as the audience begins to settle in. The writer sits in his seat next to Camille, and the writer notes that the Comic Opera is truly a magnificent place, full of features that make the theatrical experience even more special.

The main area of the Comic Opera is the performance hall, where the shows take place. The room has been masterfully designed to ensure optimum acoustics and excellent visibility for the audience. Its sloping audience allows spectators to have a clear view of the stage, making the experience even more immersive and exciting.

The stage, the heart of the theater, is where artists bring their performances to life. It can be equipped with elaborate sets, dazzling scenery, special effects, and even a sophisticated lift system that brings a unique magic to productions held there.

In addition, the performance hall is surrounded by balconies and boxes, offering different seating options for the audience. The balconies are raised areas with comfortable seats, offering a privileged view of the stage. The boxes, small private compartments with seats, are perfect for smaller groups who want a more intimate experience.

Just below the stage is the orchestral pit, the area where the orchestra positions itself to play during performances. The pit's strategic position allows the music to blend harmoniously with the stage performance, creating a unique and exciting synergy.

Another charming detail is the painted ceiling, a feature that some operas have. These ceilings are true works of art, often depicting mythological and allegorical scenes. They add a fascinating artistic dimension to the interior of the theater, leaving spectators in awe as they appreciate the beauty and creativity of these paintings.

The Comic Opera at Salle Favart, as an outstanding cultural institution, is much more than just a performance venue. It is a place where music, opera, and comedy come together to provide the audience with a unique and memorable theatrical experience.

However, the curtains close and the lights go out in the hall, beginning the play "Cyrano de Bergerac". Camille and Luiz are attentive, immersed in the magical atmosphere of the theater, ready to dive into the captivating story that is about to unfold before their eyes.

The plot takes place in 17th-century France, and the main characters soon come to life on stage. Cyrano de Bergerac, the talented poet, swordsman, and soldier with his prominent nose, arouses the audience's compassion and curiosity. His insecurity about his appearance contrasts with his skill and courage, making him a complex and fascinating protagonist.

The story unfolds around the love triangle between Cyrano, the beautiful Roxane, and the young cadet Christian. Cyrano's unrequited passion for Roxane creates an emotional dilemma, but despite suffering in silence, he decides to help Christian win her over, revealing his genius by writing love letters on his friend's behalf. This interaction brings a mixture of emotions to the stage, with touching and amusing moments.

Luiz notes that the play touches on universal themes, such as the search for true inner beauty amid issues of physical appearance and the transformative power of true love. Cyrano's journey is an ode to courage, loyalty, and sacrifice, which touches the audience's heart deeply.

As the plot unfolds, thrilling twists and turns, spectacular duels, and poetic dialogues hold the attention of everyone in the audience, including Camille and Luiz, who watch the magic of the theater unfold before them.

The famous balcony scene, where Cyrano declares his love for Roxane in the name of Christian, is a moment of pure eloquence and emotion, leaving the audience enraptured by the beauty of words and the power of love.

"Cyrano de Bergerac" transcends time and geographical barriers, touching the human essence in a profound and universal way. Edmond

Rostand created a literary masterpiece that continues to thrill and inspire, arousing the admiration of viewers and readers over the years.

Camille and Luiz, immersed in this unique theatrical experience, share meaningful glances, recognizing the greatness of the play they are witnessing. The atmosphere of the theater is enveloping, and the two enjoy every moment of this celebration of the power of poetry and true love, which touches their souls deeply.

After the thrilling performance, the theater lights come back on and Luiz and Camille, wrapped up in the excitement of the moment, stand up to warmly applaud all the cast members who took part in the play. Camille, with a smile on her face, turns to Luiz and anxiously asks if he enjoyed the performance. Luiz, still delighted with the theatrical experience, replies enthusiastically that he loved it, confessing that it was a completely new story for him, something he had never experienced before.

The two of them leave the theater in ecstasy, sharing the enthusiasm and emotion of the moment they have just experienced. The Parisian night is just beginning, and the night sky above them is full of stars, giving the city of lights a romantic atmosphere.

As they walk through the streets of Paris, Luiz and Camille enjoy the magic of the night, enjoying each other's company and sharing laughter and *lively conversation. Around every corner, they find a new surprise, a discovery to be made in the city that breathes history and culture.*

And then, in an instant, Luiz spots an Italian restaurant whose name, Mori Venice Bar, evokes images of the enchanting region of Venice. The restaurant's façade is warm, inviting, and full of details reminiscent of Venetian culture.

Without hesitation, the two decide to enter and are greeted with warm hospitality. The atmosphere is cozy, with tables adorned with plaid tablecloths and candles that gently illuminate the space, creating a romantic and intimate atmosphere.

The menu features dishes reminiscent of Venice's rich cuisine, with fresh pasta, tasty risottos, and fresh seafood. The dining experience is a true journey for the palate, with authentic flavors that transport Luiz and Camille directly to sunny Italy.

Mancini settles into his chair and orders a Coke to soften the effects of the wine. Camille, for her part, orders a delicious strawberry drink with orange liqueur, looking for a refreshing and tasty combination.

As they sip their drinks, Camille curiously asks Luiz where he is staying in the city. With a smile, Luiz replies that he is staying at the iconic Ritz Hotel. Camille, surprised, asks him how he managed to book a room there, as the hotel is known for being one of the most luxurious and exclusive in Paris. Luiz tells her that he had the opportunity to choose one of the available suites and opted for the one he liked best. However, he admits that the experience came at a considerable price, filled with several zeros, but it was worth it to experience Paris from a new and inspiring perspective.

With the menu in hand, Luiz calls the waiter over to order. Mancini chooses the tasty Risotto Mori, a combination of Vialone Nano risotto from the Abbesses Presidio "Slow Food" with green asparagus, peas, zucchini flowers, and robiola d'alpeggio cheese cream.

Camille opts for the Carabinieri, a delicious tagliatelle with poached eggs and real langoustines, in a matelote with lightly peppered tomatoes, finished with basil and fresh herbs.

The dishes chosen promise a fine dining experience, full of authentic flavors. While waiting for the dishes to arrive, Luiz and Camille share their experiences, laughter, and stories, establishing a strong connection.

The restaurant, with its warm and elegant atmosphere, provides the perfect setting for this magical evening in Paris. The atmosphere is full of charm and sophistication, perfectly matching the charming company and delicious dishes they are about to taste.

As the conversation flows and the dishes are served, Luiz and Camille allow themselves to be immersed in a truly exceptional culinary experience, appreciating every aroma, taste, and texture.

After a delicious meal, they pay the bill and leave the restaurant. Camille, with a captivating gaze, holds Luiz's hand gently and suggests:

"It would be great to walk through the Tuileries Gardens to the Jardin du Carrousel in front of the Louvre. The view from the park to the Louvre Museum at night, with the lights on, is one of the most beautiful things you can see in Paris."

Luiz, enchanted by the idea and the moment, replies:

"Sure, that could be a great idea. Let's go."

The two of them walk together through the city, enjoying the unique atmosphere that Paris offers at night. The glow of the lights and the magic of the illuminated streets create a sense of enchantment and romance around them.

As they approach the Tuileries Gardens, Luiz and Camille indulge in the beauty of the landscape, observing the trees and flowers in the moonlight. They then enter the Tuileries Gardens at night, enveloped by the enchanting atmosphere that takes over the place when the sun goes down.

The lights of the lanterns spread a soft, golden glow, giving the scenery a romantic and poetic aura. The landscape is transformed, and the paths that were once traveled by crowds of visitors now become quieter, providing an intimate moment for Luiz and Camille.

Strolling through the labyrinth of colors and scents, they are immersed in a unique and unforgettable experience. The carefully designed flower beds seem to form a multicolored carpet that invites them to explore every detail. The ornate fountains spread a soft, relaxing sound, accompanying them with every step they take.

The majestic cypresses and plane trees, with their branches stretching towards the sky, cast shadows that dance in the wind, creating a magical and enigmatic atmosphere. Around every corner, a marble statue seems to come to life, telling stories of mythological figures and characters from French history.

The Grand Canal, reflecting the night sky, becomes a mirror of calm waters that invites contemplation. As they walk along its banks, Luiz and Camille are enveloped by a sense of peace and harmony, as if they were in a fairytale setting.

The benches strategically positioned along the path offer them a moment to rest and enjoy the surrounding landscape. Sitting together, they watch the people still strolling through the park, enjoying moments of relaxation and leisure.

The Tuileries Gardens, despite being a historic place full of grandeur, also embrace the everyday life of Paris. Groups of friends laugh and chat as they share a picnic under the stars, while children run around enthusiastically, creating memories that will remain etched in their minds forever.

As Luiz and Camille make their way through the park, they feel the atmosphere steeped in French history and tradition, a setting that has witnessed so many defining moments of the monarchy and Parisian society. They find themselves enveloped by a sense of awe and wonder at such beauty.

When they finally reach the Jardin du Carrousel, facing the Louvre, they are faced with a breathtaking view of the famous museum.

Camille gracefully sits down on the soft grass and invites Luiz to do the same, creating a moment of serenity and connection between them. Luiz follows her invitation and settles down next to her, feeling the soft texture of the grass under his fingers. The surroundings take on a magical aura under the moonlight, and the breathtaking view of the Louvre Museum enchants Luiz.

The Louvre, majestic and imposing, stands before them in all its splendor. The lights carefully arranged around the structure create a soft, enveloping illumination, highlighting the architectural beauty of the building. The classical façade, with its wealth of detail, seems to come alive in the evening light as if it were telling ancient stories to those who gaze upon it.

The famous glass Pyramid, a modern icon that contrasts with the grandeur of the Louvre, is also illuminated and shines like a diamond in the center of the courtyard. The combination of historic architecture and contemporary design gives the site a unique atmosphere, symbolizing the connection between past and present.

The lights that frame the Louvre and the Pyramid cast a soft glow over the surroundings, highlighting the ornamental details of the building and creating a scene worthy of a fairy tale. The reflection of the lights in the calm waters of the nearby lake adds even more charm to the landscape, making it even more magical.

As the evening progresses, the shadows cast by the surrounding trees and statues create an intimate and romantic atmosphere. Camille and Luiz, sitting side by side, enjoy the moment in soft silence, admiring the magnificence of the Louvre and the beauty that surrounds it.

The two of them are transported to a dreamlike setting where history, art, and nature come together in a symphony of beauty and serenity. The Jardin du Carrousel, framing this enchanting view, becomes the perfect place to share special moments and create unforgettable memories. The lights adorning the Louvre and the Pyramid dance gently as the night breeze passes by, adding a touch of magic to the atmosphere.

While the two of them were immersed in the breathtaking beauty of the Tuileries Gardens and the magnificent view of the Louvre illuminated at night, Camille was preparing to share her impressions of that magical place. However, before she could say a word, something unexpected happened. An overwhelming impulse takes hold of Luiz, driven by an intense and inexplicable passion, he approaches Camille and kisses her.

The moment is charged with overwhelming emotions, and Camille is momentarily unresponsive. However, as the kiss deepens and passion takes over, she surrenders to that moment of intimacy and connection. It seems that time around them has stopped, creating a space of their own, isolated from the outside world.

The kiss is like a burning flame that ignites between them, a fusion of deep and inexpressible feelings that find a way of communicating through that passionate gesture. Every touch, every caress is an expression of affection and desire, as if the energy of the universe were conspiring to bring them together at that moment.

The Tuileries Gardens and the Louvre disappear from view, and the world around them becomes a distant mist. The only thing that matters is each other's presence, the sensation of their hands touching, and the sweetness of their lips meeting again in a passionate kiss.

Camille feels enveloped by a warm, thrilling intensity, a connection that transcends words and goes deep into her heart. She lets herself be carried away by the magic of the moment, by the power of passion and the mutual attraction that unites them.

Mancini, his eyes shining with love and emotion, looks deep into Camille's eyes and whispers the words that have been in her heart for so long:

"I love you"

The expression is simple, but carries a deep and true meaning, as if he were revealing his entire soul.

In this moment of passion and intimacy, they connect in a way that transcends reality, as if their hearts were beating in unison, in perfect harmony. They find themselves vulnerable but also strengthened by the courage to give themselves over to love.

It's as if all the stars in the sky align to create that unique and special moment, where the world around them becomes a blur, and the only thing that matters is the intense feeling that unites them.

The Tuileries Gardens, a silent witness to this love story, seem to whisper secrets to the wind as if they were sharing the joy and beauty of that sublime moment.

And there, under the starry sky of Paris, Camille and Luiz discover that love is a powerful force that brought them together on that magical night, and the magic of the city of lights only intensifies the depth of their emotions

The Frenchwoman, still a little surprised by the unexpected kiss, finds words to express her feelings:

"That's something unexpected..."

While she processes the moment, Luiz, with his hand behind his head, seems to reflect on what has just happened. The silence between them is filled with the pulsating emotions and magical atmosphere of the City of Lights.

Without hurrying, they decide to stay there a little longer, lying on the grass, looking up at the starry sky, holding hands. Luiz admires the beauty of the moment and the city around them, and can't help but agree with Camille:

"Paris is a jewel in the world."

Time seems to stretch as they share that unique moment, a deep connection that transcends words. Every second is like a poetic sigh, a moment that seemed not to belong to the real world, but to an enchanted dream.

After a while, they got up and Luiz, looking at his watch, realized that it was already late at night, around 1:07 in the morning. The city still shone with the lights on all around them, but the time was already announcing that dawn was approaching.

Camille, aware of the time, said it was time to leave. Luiz agrees with her, but before they say goodbye, they embrace, sealing the moment with tenderness. Camille kisses Luiz and, in a soft voice, says:

"See you later, writer..."

She then walks on her way home, while Luiz stands there, watching her go with his heart warmed by the emotions of the evening. The feeling of connection and enchantment remains with him.

The writer walks back to his hotel, his mind full of emotions. The streets of Paris seem to whisper stories and secrets, and the city shines with an even more intense charm after that night of passion and discovery.

Luiz arrives at the imposing entrance to the hotel, and as he enters the lobby, he greets the receptionists and the concierge with a polite smile. At that time of night, the hotel's atmosphere is very calm and quiet, in contrast to the frenetic movement usually experienced in the morning or afternoon.

He walks up the elegant staircase, appreciating the beauty of the hotel's architecture, until he reaches his suite. As he enters the room, he is greeted by a pleasant surprise: a bottle of red wine, probably chosen especially for him, sits in the living room, accompanied by a box of chocolates. A note from the concierge, in his impeccable handwriting, thanks him for his stay and offers a touch of affection by informing him that a jar of strawberry cheesecake ice cream is in the room's fridge.

Luiz is pleased with the hotel's kindness and attention in providing him with a complimentary dessert. He takes the pot of ice cream, opens the fridge, and savors each spoonful, enjoying the sweet and refreshing taste on his palate.

Satisfied and relaxed, Luiz sits down in the living room, comfortably ensconced on one of the luxurious sofas. He observes the dazzling landscape in front of him: the iconic Opéra Garnier, majestic and illuminated, adorning the city with its impeccable architecture. The night lights give Paris a special glow, creating a magical and romantic atmosphere.

While contemplating the spectacular view, Luiz's thoughts turn to Camille, the woman he met that night and who left an indelible mark on his heart. He replays every detail of their meeting, the moments of passion and joy they shared.

The city of Paris, which had already captivated him since his arrival, now takes on an even deeper meaning.

As Luiz continues to contemplate the splendid night view of Paris, a feeling of melancholy and regret begins to take hold of his heart. The memory of that magical night with Camille is accompanied by a deep sense of loss, as he hasn't caught up with her and fears that he may never be able to meet her again. The idea that those moments of passion and complicity may have been ephemeral and fleeting disturbs him, making him wonder if he made an irreparable mistake.

He remembers the glances they exchanged, the lively conversations, the smiles they shared, and now the uncertainty of meeting her again seems to haunt him. In the midst of so many thoughts, Luiz wonders why he didn't ask for her contact details, why he didn't get a phone number, an e-mail address, or any way of maintaining the bond that had been established between them.

The feeling that the chance of meeting her again has slipped through his fingers like fine, delicate sand is suffocating.

However, amid his anguish, Luiz realizes that there is something in his trouser pocket, a small object that seems to have gone unnoticed by him. He pulls the stiff paper out of his pocket and, on taking a closer look, recognizes Camille's delicate handwriting: her professional contact card. A wave of relief and hope runs through his body, and a genuine smile forms on his lips.

The discovery of this card represents a chance, a possibility to keep the flame of that unique encounter alive. Luiz leans back in the living room chair, holding the card carefully as if it were a precious treasure. He feels grateful for this second chance that fate has given him and promises himself that, this time, he won't let the opportunity to get to know Camille better slip away, to unravel the mysteries that surround her, and, who knows, to write a new story alongside her.

The relief of knowing that he hasn't lost her for good brings a sense of renewed hope. Luiz now sees a light at the end of the tunnel, a chance to experience something special with the woman who left such a deep mark on his heart. He feels determined not to let this chance slip away again because, after all, fate has presented him with a new opportunity to experience the romance that blossomed on that magical night in Paris.

While the city shines with its lights, Luiz feels the same glow ignite within him, a flame that drives him to seek out the one who has become his new muse, his source of inspiration, his passion. With Camille's contact card in his hands, he now knows that he is not alone on this journey.

After enjoying dessert, Luiz Mancini decides it's time to relax a little before indulging in the sweet rest of the Parisian night. He takes a shower, allowing the hot water to fall on his body like a revitalizing rain that washes away not only his physical tiredness but also the worries in his mind.

When he gets out of the shower, Mancini wraps himself in a soft towel and lies down on the bed, which is as comfortable as a warm hug. The bed is the perfect refuge for his weary soul, and he feels grateful to have such a cozy place to rest in such an exuberant city. The lights of Paris still shine outside the window, like an invitation to explore some more, but he knows he needs to recharge his batteries to make the most of every moment.

His eyes are heavy with fatigue and his mind is still filled with memories of last night, Luiz lets himself drift off into the sleep that is slowly taking over his body. The emotions of the day, the unexpected encounters, the shared passion, everything seems to merge into a whirlwind of sensations as he plunges into the world of dreams.

In the comfort of that bed, Luiz finds himself surrounded by a peaceful and serene atmosphere, as if he were in a private refuge amidst the hustle and bustle of the city. The distant music of the cars and the gentle murmur of the wind seem to lull him to sleep, and he surrenders to the comforting darkness that spreads over him.

After that magical encounter with Camille, which touched Luiz's heart deeply, the two met again and again over the course of several days and weeks. The connection between them only seemed to grow with each meeting, and they soon became great confidants and mutual support in their decisions. They shared their experiences, their dreams, their anxieties, and their joys as if they had known each other for years.

Luiz became more and more enchanted by Camille's captivating personality, her intelligence, her sense of humor, and her passion for life. He realized that being around her inspired him in ways he had never felt before. And, despite being an experienced writer, Luiz also noticed that Camille's presence helped him see Paris from a new perspective, giving him a wealth of detail and nuance to his stories. He also recorded his love experiences with Camille, his adventures in the Parisian streets, and the charms of the landscapes he discovered.

However, Luiz also realized that, amidst all the sightseeing and moments of shared passion, he still hadn't fully dedicated himself to exploring his creative side for the next book he wanted to write. He knew he needed to find a balance between his personal life and his writing career.

Although Luiz was familiar with some of the important sights in Paris and the surrounding countryside, he knew there was still much more to be explored. He wanted to delve into the lesser-known streets, the forgotten stories, and the landscapes that were rarely captured by the tourist gaze. He wanted to dive into the heart of Paris to find the essence of the city and use it as a backdrop for his next work.

With a heavy heart, but determined, Luiz shared his feelings with Camille. He explained that he needed a few days to devote himself fully to his writing and that, unfortunately, this would mean a little less time together. Camille, understanding and encouraging, supported his decision, knowing that art and creativity were also essential to him.

With exactly 1 month and 15 days to go until the end of his stay at the Hotel Ritz in Paris, Luiz woke up with a sparkle of enthusiasm in his eyes. That day looked promising, as he had decided to explore a new neighborhood in Paris, the charming 7th arrondissement. The sun was shining in the sky, and Luiz knew it would be a perfect day to get lost in the Parisian streets and discover new wonders.

He sat at the breakfast table in the hotel's elegant restaurant and enjoyed the delicious aroma of the freshly baked croissant. While enjoying the taste of coffee and French delicacies, he decides to let Camille know about his plans for the day. Picking up his cell phone, he sends her a message with a smile on his lips, sharing the news:

"Bonjour, Camille! Today is a special day as I've decided to explore the charming 7th arrondissement of Paris. I'm sure I'll find many delightful surprises there. I'm going to venture through the streets, appreciate the architecture, discover the hidden secrets and, of course, carry you in my heart every step of the way. I hope all is well there and that we can meet up soon to share another exciting journey together. À bientôt!"

With a feeling of excitement, Luiz finishes his breakfast and leaves the hotel. He takes the metro and is soon in the 7th arrondissement, ready to unveil the wonders the region has to offer.

The writer decides to start his exploration of the 7th arrondissement by the charming Rue Saint-Dominique. This charming street is known as the backbone of the district, connecting three of Paris' most iconic monuments: the

Musée d'Orsay to the east, the Invalides complex, and, in the end, the majestic Champ de Mars with the imposing Eiffel Tower in the background.

As he walks along the curving length of Rue Saint-Dominique, Luiz comes across a charming scene. Locals come and go, greeting each other with smiles and animated conversations. The movement is constant, but at the same time tranquil, as if time runs at its own pace in this picturesque part of Paris.

He is enchanted by the many stores and stores that fill the street. Delicious boulangeries and patisseries display their tempting windows full of freshly baked bread, golden croissants, and irresistible pastries. The scent of fresh bread hangs in the air, awakening the senses and whetting Luiz's appetite.

As he goes along, he notices elegant clothing boutiques, where French fashion is displayed in all its splendor. The fruit and vegetable sellers offer a variety of vibrant colors, reminiscent of a true painter's palette. Luiz can't resist and decides to buy a box of juicy raspberries, knowing that they will be the perfect accompaniment to his day of exploration.

As he strolls along Rue Saint-Dominique, he also notices that the street is a real showcase of everyday Parisian life. Elegant beauty salons and architecture studios are dotted around, catering to the needs and desires of the local community. It's as if the street is a reflection of the many facets of Parisian life, capturing the essence of the city in its various manifestations.

In addition to the shops, Luiz comes across several good restaurants and bistros along the way. The delicious aroma of French delicacies mixes with the welcoming atmosphere of the establishments, inviting passers-by to enjoy a pleasant meal.

At the end of his pleasant walk along Rue Saint-Dominique, Mancini decides to head for a place steeped in history and relevance: the Musée de l'Armée. The museum, which is part of the Les Invalides complex, houses one of the largest collections of military objects in the world. Here, swords, weapons, and armor are harmoniously arranged alongside models and maps that trace the evolution of warfare from prehistoric times to the Second World War. When he enters the museum, Luiz is faced with a veritable immersion in military history, with memorabilia from the era of Napoleon featuring prominently, but also exhibits of medieval, Renaissance, and Asian militias, which tell various stories of battles and strategies.

In an environment full of objects that recall great moments in humanity, Luiz feels intrigued as he analyzes the cultural and war wealth that unfolds before his eyes. Each piece there has its own story, a meaning that blends with the course of world history. The grandeur of the collection and the diversity of periods and cultures represented in the museum captivate your writer's mind, awakening in Luiz a desire to capture in words the sensations and emotions that the visit brings.

On leaving the Musée de l'Armée, Luiz also decides to enter the Les Invalides complex itself, a monumental 17th-century architectural complex commissioned by Louis XIV to provide accommodation and hospital care for veterans of France's wars. The place is permeated by an aura of respect and gratitude for the heroes who fought for the colors of their homeland.

The history of the complex takes on even more significance when you learn that, after Napoleon's abdication in 1815, 5,000 veterans of his Grande Armée sought refuge in Les Invalides. Later, in 1840, Napoleon found his final resting place there, where his body was transferred to the domed church, appropriately called the Eglise du Dome.

The weight of history is felt in every corner, enveloping Luiz in a feeling of reverence for those who were part of those remarkable times.

With the raspberries deliciously savored, Luiz continues on his way towards the Champ de Mars, enjoying the frenetic movement of the city during the day, in contrast to the tranquility of the night. The cityscape changes along the way, with busy traffic and people hurrying along the streets and sidewalks.

Arriving at the Champ de Mars, he is enchanted by the vast green space that stretches out before his eyes. It's a great place to walk around and explore, and Luiz feels enveloped by the historical aura of the place. As he walks around, he admires the elegant apartments that line the park, with their breathtaking views of the Eiffel Tower. It's as if he can feel the pulse of history in every corner, imagining the battles that took place over the centuries, when the Roman Legions defeated the Parisii in 52 BC or when the Parisians triumphed over the Viking invaders in 886 AD.

This feeling of being plunged into the past is intensified by remembering that in 1790, Charles Talleyrand, a popular French bishop, organized one of the first Bastille celebrations in this very field. Luiz feels connected to the generations who have walked there, absorbing the energy and history that permeate the place.

Previously, the Champ de Mars was used as a military parade ground by the nearby military school. However, over the years, the space became a place of celebration and public gatherings, hosting several international exhibitions in 1867, 1878, 1889, 1900, and 1937. These events have contributed to the evolution of the site's history, turning it into a cultural icon of Paris.

Walking along the Champ de Mars is a real experience of immersion in the city's past and present. Luiz feels enveloped by the festive yet reflective atmosphere that permeates the park. Every step he takes seems to echo the historical events that took place there, while at the same time, he sees the space being enjoyed by visitors and residents of Paris, coming together for moments of leisure and conviviality.

While Luiz records every detail of his visit in his little diary, he sets off towards the most famous tourist attraction in France and one of the most iconic in the world, the majestic Eiffel Tower. No itinerary through the 7th Arrondissement can be considered complete without the inclusion of this iconic symbol of Paris, which has become an enduring representation of the city.

As he approaches the site, he is transported to the year 1889, a time when the world was at the height of scientific and technological progress. This decade was marked by impressive achievements, such as the first cars, the telephone, and electric lighting. And, at the apex of this innovative scenario, the grandiose Eiffel Tower appeared.

Built to commemorate the centenary of the French Revolution and as the centerpiece of the 1889 International Exhibition, the tower stood out as the tallest structure in the world at the time. Its grandeur and architectural ingenuity not only amazed Parisians and visitors but also symbolized the human capacity to dream of possibilities and explore the limits of the imagination.

Over the years, the Eiffel Tower has become one of the main symbols of France and Paris itself. Today, it is the most visited monument in the world, attracting tourists from all over. However, with fame comes demand, and long queues can be an inconvenience for visitors. Aware of this, Luiz decides to follow a valuable piece of advice: avoid the crowds and endless queues by opting for a skip-the-line tour of the Eiffel Tower.

This choice gives him the opportunity to get to the top quickly and enjoy the breathtaking view of Paris without wasting precious moments waiting. Luiz knows that in order to live this unique experience to the full, it's important to enjoy every moment without worrying about queues and wasted time.

At the foot of the Eiffel Tower, he feels small in the face of its grandeur, but at the same time inspired by the human capacity to create and build wonders like this. With every step he takes towards the top, he is enchanted by the breathtaking view that unfolds, taking in all the beauty of Paris, from the beautiful rooftops of its buildings to the majestic monuments that dot the skyline.

As he contemplates the city from above, Luiz can't help but feel that he is witnessing a living painting, with its unique colors, shapes, and movements. The Eiffel Tower becomes a meeting point between the past and the present, an imposing structure that carries with it the history of Paris and humanity.

From the top of the iconic Eiffel Tower, Luiz is faced with a breathtaking view. The sun is shining brightly, illuminating every corner of the city and making Paris sparkle like a rare diamond. From that height, people look like little ants in a hive, scurrying through the streets and squares, each with its history and purpose.

The vastness of the Parisian skyline stretches out before Luiz's eyes, and he feels immersed in a true visual spectacle. The roofs of the buildings stretch out in all directions, creating a symphony of shapes and colors. The beautiful avenues and elegant boulevards trace paths that lead to magical places where history and modernity merge in enchanting harmony.

Each monument and landmark stands out like sparkling jewels amidst the cityscape. The majestic Notre-Dame Cathedral, the grandiose Opera Garnier, and the imposing Louvre all bear silent witness to Paris' rich history and culture. Luiz feels part of this history as if every part of the city is imbued with memories and emotions that echo down the centuries.

The Eiffel Tower itself is an architectural masterpiece, and Luiz marvels at its structural elegance. Every detail seems meticulously planned, from the graceful lines of the stairs to the elaborate arches that support the structure. He feels connected to the genius of Gustave Eiffel, the man behind this masterpiece, and feels a deep admiration for the human ingenuity that made this vision a reality.

As he watches the city from above, Luiz feels a mixture of emotions bubbling up inside him. The joy and excitement of being in such a magical and inspiring place is accompanied by a sense of serenity and peace. The hustle and bustle of the city below seems distant and insignificant as he surrenders to the tranquillity of the moment.

The gentle breeze caresses Luiz's face, bringing with it the characteristic scents of Paris: the perfume of the flowers in the gardens, the tantalizing aroma of the cafés and boulangeries, and the slight touch of history and culture that permeates the air. You feel enveloped by a unique atmosphere, where past and present intertwine in an enchanting dance.

Descending from the Eiffel Tower at around 3:50 p.m., Luiz heads to his next destination: the Palais Bourbon - National Assembly. This majestic palace, built in 1728 for the Duchess of Bourbon, Louise Françoise de Bourbon, captivates the writer with its imposing Greek Renaissance façade that reflects the opulence of the Église de La Madeleine, on the other side of the River Seine. Today, it is where the Assemblée Nationale meets to make important political decisions.

On arriving at the Place du Palais-Bourbon, built in 1776, Luiz is greeted by the palace's grand main entrance, which offers a spectacular view of the inner courtyard. Although access to the tours inside the building is organized in advance by the elected deputies, he admires the magnificent History of Civilization painted by Delacroix on the ceiling of the library, a true artistic treasure.

After this experience, Luiz decides to head to the Rodin Museum, located to the east of Les Invalides, near the Place du Palais-Bourbon. He marvels at the architecture of the elegant 17th and 18th-century hotels that adorn the area, especially the Hôtel de Biron, where the renowned sculptor Auguste Rodin lived and worked until he died in 1917. Today, this building houses the Rodin Museum, which has become a haven for artistic expression.

Luiz enters the museum and is immediately enchanted by Rodin's works that occupy the delicately designed spaces. Taking advantage of the fact that the museum is not very large, he has the chance to appreciate each sculpture in detail, reflecting on the artist's genius and his relationship with the also talented sculptor Camille Claudel.

Exploring the museum's gardens, Luiz feels a deep connection with art and nature, which combine harmoniously in the environment. The sculptures amidst the greenery exude an aura of life and emotion, inviting you to immerse yourself in Rodin's creative world and contemplate the stories that each work carries.

At the end of his visit to the Rodin Museum, the writer continues his cultural exploration and heads to the Quai Branly Museum, a relatively new addition to the Paris museum scene, which opened in 2006. The museum houses a rich collection of African, Asian, Oceania and Native American arts and civilizations, offering visitors a unique experience of immersion in different cultures and traditions.

When he enters the Quai Branly Museum, Luiz is impressed by the diversity of the exhibitions, which reveal the artistic and historical riches of these continents. He marvels at the skill and creativity of the artists who created the works on display, which tell stories of times gone by and narrate the lives of different peoples and communities.

As he explores the museum's rooms, Luiz comes across special exhibitions on a variety of themes, from folk art to the representation of human forms in *native art. One of the most recent exhibitions, on the primitive influences on Picasso's work, draws his attention because of his fascination with the work of the renowned Spanish painter and his curiosity to understand how distant cultures influenced his artistic style.*

Each section of the museum is carefully designed to provide an immersive experience, and Luiz feels transported to different parts of the world without leaving Paris. He looks in detail at African masks, Asian ceramics, artifacts from Oceania, and sculptures from Native American civilizations. Each piece is a window into a unique cultural universe and, at the same time, reflects the rich human diversity that permeates the planet.

In the middle of this cultural journey through Paris, Mancini heads to another museum that is a real treasure for art lovers: the Musée d'Orsay. Competing with the renowned Louvre for the title of the best museum in the city, the Musée d'Orsay is Luiz's favorite. Formerly a magnificent train station from the turn of the 20th century, the museum was transformed in 1986 into a dazzling showcase of 19th-century art and culture.

Upon entering the Musée d'Orsay, Luiz is immediately enveloped by the enchanting atmosphere that emanates from the space, which is filled with masterpieces by renowned artists who have marked the history of art. The museum's collection spans the period from Romanticism to the birth of modern art, a veritable journey through time through the evolution of artistic expressions.

The Musée d'Orsay's collection houses an impressive collection of works by the Impressionist masters, including the talented Manet, Monet, van Gogh, Degas, Pissarro, Renoir, and Berthe Morisot, among others. Each canvas is a treat for the eyes, with vivid and expressive brushstrokes that capture light and life in dazzling colors.

Of all these renowned artists, Claude Monet is the painter who most enchants Luiz. The way Monet portrays landscapes, gardens, and everyday scenes is truly exceptional. Looking at the artist's works, Luiz is transported to a universe of vibrant colors and strokes that seem to come to life and move before his eyes.

From a distance, Monet's paintings present an impression of realism that can deceive the eye, but when you get closer, Luiz realizes the genius behind the seemingly unpretentious brushstrokes, creating a sense of magic and mystery in each canvas.

Through the impressionist brushstrokes, Luiz feels connected to the emotions and sensations that the artists were trying to convey, and understands the quest to capture the essence of the moment, the light, and the colors that make each canvas a unique experience.

After absorbing the beauty and charm of the Musée d'Orsay, Luiz leaves the museum with his mind full of thoughts and emotions awakened by the works of art he has contemplated, especially those by Claude Monet, the painter who most amazed him. With his little diary in hand, he writes down his sensations and reflections, trying to capture in words the magic he felt when observing each of the impressionist artist's lively and expressive brushstrokes.

Thirsty after his intense artistic experience, Luiz decides to go to the Fontaine de Mars, a place that can satisfy both his desire for water and his hunger. This independent fountain, built by Henri Beauvarlet, carries with it the history of a bygone era, when it was surrounded by a bucolic grove of poplar trees. Even after the area was transformed into a square, the fountain remains a beautiful testament to the past, a symbol of resistance to time.

As Luiz approaches the Fontaine de Mars, he comes across a bas-relief depicting Hygeia, the goddess of health, offering a drink to Mars, the god of war. This harmonious mythological image seems to echo the harmony he felt in Monet's brushstrokes and in the whole artistic atmosphere that Paris gave him.

While he's quenching his thirst at the fountain, Luiz can't resist going into the bistro of the same name, La Fontaine de Mars. The aroma of delicious French dishes envelops him, making his decision to have lunch or dinner there an easy one. This charming bistro has been popular since 1908 and carries on its walls stories of unforgettable meals, including those of the Obama family during their visit to Paris in 2009.

After satisfying his hunger at the Fontaine de Mars, Luiz decides to take a short break to enjoy the city in all its splendor. The lights of Paris begin to come on, painting a magical scene that envelops the entire atmosphere of the city. The iconic monuments shine like stars, and the Eiffel Tower shines majestically on the horizon. Amid this romantic setting, Luiz feels grateful to be experiencing such special moments in the City of Lights.

In the evening, the writer returns to the Hotel Ritz to prepare for dinner with Camille. Luiz's heart is bursting with emotion and he can't wait to share with her the experiences he's had while exploring Paris' charming 7th arrondissement.

As they meet in the hotel restaurant, the complicit glances and smiles exchanged between Luiz and Camille demonstrate the connection they have. As they enjoy an exquisite meal, Luiz shares with Camille all the details of his day of exploration. He describes the beauty and charm of the Rue

Saint-Dominique, the Impressionist works of art at the Musée d'Orsay, and the sensations he felt when looking at Monet's paintings.

Camille listens attentively to Luiz's every word, her eyes shining with admiration for his passion for art and the city that surrounds it. The exchange of experiences and the complicity between them only strengthen the bonds that have been established with each meeting.

After dinner, the couple retire to the hotel suite, where the intimate and romantic atmosphere seems to reflect the glow of the city outside. Together, they surrender to the charm of Paris and indulge in the love that grows between them.

Under the Starry Mantle of Paris

When that unforgettable day in the 7th arrondissement of Paris ended, Camille and Luiz's story seemed to have found its bearings. They went out together more often, exploring more and more of the charms of the City of Lights. However, Luiz decided to put off exploring the other district until the following week, as he wanted to enjoy Camille's company as much as possible.

That week, the pair embarked on two exciting trips together: Versailles and Mont Saint-Michel.

Versailles, one of France's most iconic destinations, turned out to be a real trip back in time. Camille and Luiz marveled at the splendor of the Palace of Versailles, once the residence of the French kings. The sumptuous interiors, gilded halls, and spectacular gardens tell the story of the French monarchy and its grand architecture. Luiz's historical curiosity led him to discover that the famous Hall of Mirrors, where important treaties and agreements have been signed throughout history, has 357 mirrors along its length, an astonishing feat for the time.

As they strolled through the gardens of Versailles, Louis and Camille felt transported to a time of splendor and elegance. The fountains and ornate sculptures created a magical and romantic atmosphere, perfect for moments together.

The next destination was Mont Saint-Michel, an architectural and natural jewel of Normandy. On arrival, Luiz and Camille were impressed by the majestic abbey at the top of the rocky island. The ascent to the abbey, surrounded by the sea during high tide, gave them a breathtaking view of the French coastline.

Luiz discovered that Mont Saint-Michel is known for its extreme tidal changes, which vary drastically according to the time of day. He found it fascinating to observe the phenomenon of the "rising of the waters", when the mountain is completely surrounded by the sea, giving the illusion that the abbey is floating on water.

Upon entering the abbey, Luiz and Camille marveled at the Gothic architecture and the medieval characteristics of the place. Luiz was impressed by the ingenious use of architecture to capture natural light and create a mystical atmosphere inside the abbey.

On both trips, Luiz and Camille shared moments of wonder and discovery.

Then, after a memorable week at Camille's side, the time came for Luiz to embark on a new exploration of Parisian charms. Aware that it would be impossible to visit all the city's districts and sites, the writer decided to prioritize the main destinations in Paris. That day, he chooses the charming 5th arrondissement as his destination.

When he wakes up, Luiz enjoys a light and healthy breakfast, accompanied by a selection of fresh fruit and a comforting lemon tea. He savors every bite, preparing for another day of discovering the city.

With renewed energy, Luiz heads to the nearest metro station, carefully choosing the line that will take him to the 5th arrondissement. He decides to take metro line 7, one of the busiest lines in the city, known for passing through many of Paris's sights and interesting neighborhoods.

As soon as he arrives at the station, Luiz gets off at the Censier-Daubenton stop, one of the most emblematic stops in the 5th arrondissement. The lively atmosphere of the area envelops him as he climbs the stairs of the station, ready to begin his journey through the district.

The 5th arrondissement is known for its cultural and intellectual wealth, housing the famous Sorbonne and other important educational centers. The narrow, picturesque streets are lined with bookshops, historic cafés, and small boutiques offering traditional, authentic French products.

Luiz Mancini decides to follow in Hemingway's footsteps in Paris of the roaring twenties and embarks on an exciting journey to visit the famous writer's favorite places. His first destination is Hemingway's first apartment in Paris, located on rue du Cardinal Lemoine.

Upon arriving on the historic street, Luiz contemplates the charming Parisian architecture, with its Haussmann-style buildings that seem to tell stories of the past. He imagines Hemingway walking along these same streets, feeling the energy and vibrancy of the city that inspired him in his writings.

The writer enters the building at 74 rue du Cardinal Lemoine and climbs the stairs that Hemingway used to walk up decades ago. On the second floor, he finds the apartment where the legendary author lived at the beginning of his literary career. The feeling of being in a place steeped in history is palpable, and Luiz connects with the creative essence that permeates the environment.

Luiz then moves on to Hemingway's other favorite places in Paris. He decides to visit the iconic Café de Flore, located on Boulevard Saint-Germain-des-Prés. The café is known for being a meeting place for intellectuals and artists of the time, and Hemingway frequented the place with his writer and poet friends. Luiz sits at one of the outdoor tables, under the famous green awning, and orders an espresso, recalling the days when great creative minds discussed ideas and shared their stories in this very place.

The next destination is the legendary Shakespeare and Company bookshop, located near Notre-Dame Cathedral.

As soon as Luiz enters the bookshop, he senses an enchanting literary atmosphere, immersed in works by classic and contemporary writers. Hemingway was a regular at Shakespeare and Company, and Luiz finds a special book that reminds him of one of the author's best-loved short stories.

In the vibrant atmosphere of the iconic Shakespeare and Company bookstore, Luiz wanders the aisles filled with books carefully lined up on dark wooden shelves.

The soft scent of paper fills the air, inviting him to explore every corner of that veritable library of literary treasures. Among the many books, he finds two titles that instantly catch his eye: a classic love story and a dramatic tale of tragedy. Luiz holds the books carefully, feeling the soft texture of the covers and the weight of the printed words waiting to be unraveled.

The story behind Shakespeare and Company is as fascinating as the works it houses. Originally founded by Sylvia Beach in 1919, the bookshop was intended to be a meeting place for writers, artists, and intellectuals of the time. At the height of the Roaring Twenties, it became a refuge for authors such as Ernest Hemingway, F. Scott Fitzgerald, and James Joyce, who frequented the establishment and debated literature, art, and philosophy.

However, the original bookshop was closed during the Second World War. It wasn't until 1951 that George Whitman reopened it in another location, maintaining the literary spirit and welcoming atmosphere that made it famous. He named it Shakespeare and Company, after Sylvia Beach's legendary bookstore.

Today, Shakespeare and Company is much more than a bookstore - it is a true literary institution and a place of pilgrimage for literature lovers from all over the world. With a unique "sleep on books" policy, the bookstore offers shelter and food to young writers and artists in exchange for a few hours of work in the store. It's definitely a place that values writers and people in need. These aspiring writers, known as "Tumbleweeds", become part of the literary community of Paris and enrich the experience of visitors with their unique stories and perspectives.

Mancini is delighted to hear these stories and learn about the legacy surrounding the bookshop. He feels as if he is immersed in a magical atmosphere, where words come to life and the imagination runs wild. It's as if Shakespeare and Company itself were embracing him, inviting him to be part of its rich literary history.

With the two books in hand, Luiz walks up to the counter, where a friendly clerk offers him a warm smile. As he pays for the books, he can't help but feel a special connection with the place, as if he were taking a piece of the bookshop's soul with him.

After leaving Shakespeare and Company, Luiz walks through the charming streets of Paris towards his next destination: the Cluny Museum. Upon entering the museum, he is immediately transported to the fascinating world of the Middle Ages. The carefully organized exhibitions offer a complete immersion in the history of the time, revealing artifacts, works of art, and artifacts of everyday life from that period.

The walls of the museum seem to whisper secrets and mysteries of times gone by as Luiz walks through the corridors filled with meticulously preserved artifacts. Medieval objects such as jewelry, weapons, costumes, and manuscripts tell the stories of knights, kings, and queens, offering a unique insight into the richness and complexity of medieval society.

One of the main attractions of the Cluny Museum is the opportunity to explore the remains of a Roman bath, which dates back to a time before the Middle Ages. The intriguing ruins allow Luiz to imagine what daily activities were like in that space of leisure and personal care, connecting him to the distant past.

After satisfying his medieval curiosity, Luiz decides to head to the Jardin des Plantes, eager to appreciate the exuberant botanical beauty that awaits. As he enters the garden, he is greeted by a wonderful green world, where a variety of exotic plants and trees stretch out before his eyes. The wrought iron greenhouses, dating from the 18th century, add a unique elegance to the setting, housing exotic plants that can withstand the climate all year round.

Luiz marvels at the beauty of the cherry trees in full bloom, creating a spectacle of colors that seems straight out of a dream. He is attracted by the delicate and soft shapes of the flowers, feeling at one with nature amidst the hustle and bustle of the city.

In the Jardin des Plantes, Luiz walks along the quiet paths, enjoying the peace and serenity that the environment offers. Birdsong and the scent of flowers fill the air, providing a moment of peace and contemplation in the midst of busy Paris.

Intrigued by the wonders of nature, Luiz couldn't miss the opportunity to explore the Grande Galerie de l'Evolution, located within the Jardin des Plantes. This museum is truly a paradise for families and wildlife lovers. Upon entering, he is immediately transported to a world of discovery, with its huge display cases showcasing more than 7,000 species that seem to come to life before his eyes.

Luiz marvels at the wealth of detail and the incredible reality of the exhibits. Animals and creatures from every continent are represented there, from majestic elephants to delicate butterflies. The feeling of being surrounded by so much wildlife is overwhelming, as if he were on a journey to the four corners of the world, exploring the most exotic and wild habitats.

As he walks through the galleries, Mancini learns about the life and habits of each species. Detailed information is laid out next to the exhibits, offering a real dive into the animal kingdom.

After seeing the information and curiosities of the animal kingdom, Luiz decides to end his visit in the 5th arrondissement, in a place that has long whispered to him promises of knowledge and culture. His steps lead him elegantly to the venerable University of La Sorbonne, the epicenter of Parisian erudition and beyond.

The history of this institution, whose roots are intertwined with the very past of the City of Lights, is like an enchanted tale of learning. Founded in the early years of the Renaissance, La Sorbonne emerged as a beacon of wisdom amid the darkness of the unknown. The enlightened minds who walked its corridors echo like whispers from the past: Voltaire, Rousseau, Curie. Every stone worn down by history seems to whisper the echoes of intellectual discussions and heated debates that have shaped intellectual thought.

Characterized by an atmosphere imbued with intellect and curiosity, La Sorbonne hosts a community of overwhelming minds, a boiling cauldron where the pursuit of knowledge is the highest purpose. Meetings under the century-old vaults resonate with arguments that shape the future, where the past is appreciated and the present is reimagined.

But it is the architecture that truly fascinates the writer. The Gothic towers stand like guardians of time, dotting the Parisian skyline with an imposing dignity. Lacy windows frame the history that pulses within the centuries-old walls, a history that awaits to be discovered and reinterpreted by each new student.

Luiz also found the university library unique. The vast, silent room where knowledge hides among the aged pages. The sun's rays, filtered through the stained glass windows, dance over the shelves, creating a spectacle of light and shadow that echoes the murmurs of the minds that have frequented it.

After his immersion in the library and the imposing passageways of the university, at around 5:43 p.m., Luiz Mancini heads for the elegant bistro

L'Epoque 81. This place, with its welcoming and nostalgic aura, brings with it the essence of gastronomic traditions, a true refuge for palates that seek comfort in the delights of the past.

L'Epoque stands out for its generous cuisine, where flavors intertwine with history in every dish served. Here, culinary craftsmanship is revered, rescuing recipes that have stood the test of time. And it is precisely the call of hunger that guides Luiz to a moment of satisfaction.

He places his order, a tomato salad with burrata and pieces of artisan bread, a combination that evokes the sunny flavors of the Mediterranean. Accompanied by fresh orange juice, his choice is as satisfying as it is undeniably authentic.

As you savor each mouthful, your eyes wander to the window, capturing the scene unfolding in the square in front of the bistro. A fountain, with water dancing under the sun

Luiz makes his way back to the Hotel Ritz after enjoying his meal in the bistro. The grandeur of the hotel stands before him like a haven of timeless elegance, reminiscent of the days when dreams were woven in gold and silver.

As soon as he enters the hotel, Luiz shares with Camille the enchantments he has discovered during the day. Luiz's eyes sparkle with enthusiasm as he recounts the stories of the university, the enchanting details of Shakespeare and Company, and the unique places in the area. Camille, attentive, absorbs his words as if she were living every moment with him.

After exchanging words and laughs with Camille, Luiz prepares to enjoy a moment of relaxation. Putting on his bathing suit with the certainty of those who master time, he heads for the hotel pool. The water sparkles invitingly under the golden lights, promising to refresh and invigorate.

After his swimming session, Luiz surrenders to the comfort of a bath, allowing the warm drops of water to run down his skin. With a serene mind, he retires to the living room of his suite, where a diary waits patiently.

Words flow from the tip of Luiz's pen as he writes down his experiences and discoveries. Each line is an attempt to capture the essence of the day, the emotions that coursed through his veins, and the ideas that danced in his mind. The diary becomes an intimate treasure, a testimony to the experiences that shape his journey.

With darkness enveloping the city, Mancini indulges in the indulgence of a refined dinner at the hotel. And then, like the curtains of a stage closing softly, he retires to bed, ready to dream of the new chapters that the coming days will bring.

A few days have passed since that memorable dinner, and Luiz finds himself once again under the irresistible spell of the City of Lights. Today, his curiosity leads him to explore the 8th arrondissement of Paris, a promising setting for discoveries and fascinating experiences.

Like a sacred ritual, Luiz starts his day with breakfast in the hotel's exquisite setting, where every delicacy looks like a gastronomic masterpiece. Camille, with whom he shares his heart, joins him for this morning moment and asks with a warm smile:

"Luiz, my dear, how have your days been?"

He then replies enthusiastically:

" Camille, every day has been a journey! The city is full of stories and life around every corner"

Their gazes meet, like two souls connected by an invisible thread. So Luiz decides to share his plan to explore the 8th arrondissement, hoping that the flame of adventure will light up her eyes:

"Today my journey takes me to the 8th arrondissement. It would be an honor to have you join me in this search for inspiration, references, and special moments..."

She pauses for a moment, her eyes searching his with tenderness, and speaks:

"Luiz, you put me off like that... It would be a pleasure to explore this magical region with you."

After the last sip of coffee, they get up from the table and leave the Hotel Ritz. Camille and Luiz decide to explore the 8th arrondissement on foot, as it's good for absorbing the essence of Paris, each step a way of connecting with the city in an intimate way. As they walk, the world around them comes to life in vivid detail. The Parisian sky on the day is a little overcast.

As the two advance, the majestic Church of la Madeleine looms before them. The church's imposing architecture seems to kiss the sky, evoking a reverence that transcends time. The beauty of this immortal structure captures Luiz and Camille's gaze, reminding them that Paris is a city where past and present coexist harmoniously.

As they continue, they pass stores that exude luxury and elegance. Hermès, with its subtly sophisticated window display, attracts curious glances. They appreciate the meticulous details that define these iconic brands, an expression of Parisian craftsmanship and aesthetics that permeate every corner of the city.

Amidst the vibrant scenery of the 8th arrondissement, Luiz and Camille share the excitement of exploring the Petit Palais - Musée des Beaux-Arts. With their curiosity burning like a flame, they immerse themselves in the details that bring out the essence of this place.

Camille, with her intimate knowledge of the city, offers some information as they approach the Petit Palais. She mentions that the museum is positioned facing the River Seine, on the majestic Alexandre III Bridge. Across the street, its more imposing brother, the Grand Palais, stretches out with its own grandeur.

Luiz, seduced by Camille's words, absorbs every detail like an apprentice hungry for knowledge. They pass through the majestic doors of the Petit Palais, a building that bears the history and splendor of the 1900 Universal Exhibition. He listens intently as Camille shares how the museum evolved to house the Musée des Beaux-Arts, a treasure trove of masterpieces that enrich the soul of the city.

As they explore the interior, Camille reminds Luiz about the stunning winter garden. An oasis of serenity where shimmering ponds reflect the sunlight, and columns adorned with mosaics tell silent stories. And, as a promise of relaxing moments, she mentions that in the warm months, sitting outside and enjoying drinks is a perfect way to take in the enchanting atmosphere of the place.

The museum, which is constantly evolving, also hosts special exhibitions that captivate the senses and invite the mind to explore new horizons. She shares that the museum recently hosted a popular exhibition on Oscar Wilde and his connection with Paris.

So after immersing themselves in the wonders of the Petit Palais, Luiz and Camille decide that their journey through Parisian beauty is not yet complete. They head for the next destination in their quest for cultural treasures, the Nissim de Camondo Museum. On the way, as their steps line up in sync, Luiz notices something that captures his attention.

A majestic statue of Charles de Gaulle stands in front of Luiz in Place Clemenceau. The square, named after the illustrious French politician Georges Clemenceau, evokes memories of a time of unification and resilience. Luiz stops for a moment, his eyes fixed on the statue, and he lets himself be enveloped by the imposing presence of a leader who left his mark on history. The statue is a silent witness to the events that shaped the nation.

When they arrive at the Nissim Museum in Camondo, their expectations are far exceeded. The rich estate, a mansion that stands next to Parc Monceau, is a tribute to the grandeur of a bygone era. This beautiful mansion was once owned by a wealthy Parisian family whose history took a tragic turn during the dark days of the Second World War. The name Camondo evokes memories of a resilient family whose son Nissim, a pioneer of the skies and war hero, left an indelible legacy.

As they enter the mansion, Luiz and Camille feel the presence of history in every corner. The collection of 18th-century furniture and objects that fill the spaces is more than just a display; it is a testimony to an era of opulence and refinement. The elegant furniture, the details, and the carefully preserved souvenirs tell the story of a family and an era that should not be forgotten.

As the sunlight dances through the windows, they leave the museum with hearts full of admiration and respect for the legacy they have found. The two now decide to go and see the Statue of Liberty's Flame, a symbol that connects two distant nations through a spirit of freedom and unity.

The Flame of the Statue of Liberty is a treasure hidden in the Pont d'Alma, on the waters of the Seine. Luiz and Camille come across a life-size replica, covered in gold leaf, which reflects the sun's rays like a promise of hope. This flame is a tribute to the torch that burns atop the Statue of Liberty in New York, a presence that evokes immigration, freedom, and the pursuit of the American dream.

Luiz says that the monument was the result of a campaign promoted by the International Herald Tribune to celebrate the centenary of its publication in Paris. The flame was dedicated in 1988, a landmark of the union between cultures and nations.

The interaction with the Flame of Liberty serves as a bridge to one of the most emblematic sites in Paris: the Arc de Triomphe. The couple is carried away by the emotion that this historical icon evokes as they make their way through the streets that lead to this majestic monument.

The Champs-Elysées, the famous avenue that leads to the Arc de Triomphe, is a real spectacle for the senses. The elegant stores that line the avenue exude Parisian luxury and style. Each shop window is a window onto fashion, art, and design, a testament to the refinement that permeates every aspect of Parisian life. The pedestrians who wander along the promenade are like characters in a story, each carrying a piece of Paris with them.

The beauty of the boulevard transcends the material, as it is also home to a wealth of history and culture. The impeccable organization of the boulevard, with its rows of trees and wide sidewalks, is a testament to Paris' dedication to creating an environment that inspires awe.

As they walk along the avenue, they share the curiosities of the Champs-Elysées. Camille mentions how the avenue is the scene of festivities and celebrations, a center of social gatherings and cultural manifestations that unite the city in a web of connections.

Finally, they reach the long-awaited Arc de Triomphe, and their eyes rise to the majesty that rises before them. Luiz and Camille, as observers of history, share a moment of reverence. They feel small in front of the monument that celebrates France's achievements and pays homage to those who fought for its greatness.

Luiz and Camille climb the stairs that take them to the top of the arch, their souls vibrating with the thrill of contemplating the city from above. The panoramic view of Paris stretches out before them like a living painting, a tapestry of rooftops, monuments, and streets that echo with the life pulsing below. They share silence, a moment of deep connection where words seem redundant in the face of the magnificence unfolding before their eyes.

At the highest point of the Arc de Triomphe, while Luiz and Camille contemplate the city that stretches out before them, Camille proposes to Luiz the idea of visiting the Parc Monceau. The suggestion is met with enthusiasm, and they descend from the arch in anticipation of a new adventure.

On their way to the Parc Monceau, Luiz and Camille share moments of comfortable silence. The city that continues to surround them seems more peaceful and gentle than ever. As they reach the park, a collective sigh seems to escape their lips. The serene atmosphere and surrounding beauty welcome them like a warm embrace.

They sit down on the lush green grass, a palette of colors surrounding them. It's a moment to rest and soak up the tranquillity that the park offers. It's around 4 p.m., and the sun's rays dance gently on the leaves of the trees and plants.

The park was created in the 18th century, and commissioned by the Duke of Chartres, with a desire to create a space that embodied the charm of European landscapes. The park's history is a testament to the vision of beauty and tranquillity that Paris seeks to offer its inhabitants and visitors.

The beauty of Parc Monceau is undeniable. The harmonious blend of different landscapes, from picturesque bridges to romantic ruins, gives the park a very calm and beautiful atmosphere. The serene lake reflects the sky like a magical mirror, while the statues and architectural structures evoke a sense of timeless elegance.

At the height of their visit, Luiz and Camille surrender to the serenity that the park provides. They close their eyes for a moment, allowing the gentle breeze to caress their faces. It's an instant of connection with nature, a break from the hustle and bustle of the city and an opportunity to savor life.

Luiz slowly opens his eyes in the middle of Parc Monceau, as if waking up from a peaceful dream. He turns his attention to Camille and, with a smile, breaks the soft silence that surrounds them:

"Camille, are you hungry? Would you like something to eat?"

Camille replied promptly:
"Yes, of course! I'm starving..."

Together, they leave the serene park behind, but the sense of peace they experienced still resonates within them. They return to the Champs-Élysées, the emblematic avenue that continues to captivate their senses. With the desire to eat somewhere different, they walk in search of a place to satisfy their appetites.

As they wander, their attentive eyes search for something special. And then, like a magical scene unfolding before them, they spot a restaurant that seems to be the answer to their desires. A restaurant with a rooftop that extends into the sky, an invitation to dine with a panoramic view of the Arc de Triomphe and the city's most iconic avenue that seems to pulsate with life.

With high expectations, Luiz and Camille enter Restaurant Le W. The setting, imbued with an elegant atmosphere, seems to be an extension of the city itself. As the main characters in this scene, they approach the waiter with a curious smile. They ask the waiter if there are any vacancies on the rooftop so that they can enjoy every moment of the beautiful view.

The waiter replies with a tilt of his head, confirming that seats are available on the rooftop. They then follow the waiter towards this special area. With each step, they get closer to the opportunity to enjoy not only a meal, but also a breathtaking view of the city that enchants them.

On the rooftop, they settle down, their hearts full of gratitude for the opportunity to be in such an exceptional place. The chairs are chosen with care, providing the best possible view of the Arc de Triomphe and the avenue that stretches out like a golden carpet before them. The city, illuminated by daylight, looks like a living painting, a masterpiece that they can savor while enjoying their meal.

The menus are handed out and they share a complicit look, as if they were about to unveil a new chapter in their gastronomic adventure. A starter, main course, and dessert combo is chosen with the promise of a complete experience. Camille, with her passion for French culture, selects a rosé from the South of France as her choice of drink for the occasion.

While enjoying their meal, Luiz and Camille indulge in the taste of the dishes. A salad with olives as a starter, a selection of seafood accompanied by fish as a main course, and the tantalizing sweetness of a crème brûlée to finish.

As the meal progresses, they can't help but marvel at the beauty that surrounds them. The view from the rooftop, the Arc de Triomphe rising proudly on the horizon, the glow of the city that seems to celebrate life itself.

Dusk approaches as Luiz and Camille complete their meal on the rooftop of Restaurant Le W. The flavors still dance on their taste buds, and the feeling of gratitude for the moment shared envelops them like a warm embrace.

As the afternoon wears on, Camille makes a suggestion with a hint of enthusiasm. She suggests they visit the Basilica of the Sacred Heart in Montmartre, an invitation Luiz readily accepts.

With the sky beginning to turn shades of pink and orange, they set off on foot through the streets of Paris, intermittent raindrops beginning to fall. The rain is like a gentle touch that seems to bless their journey. Walking together, they share laughs and glances full of anticipation, each step bringing them closer to the Basilica that hangs like a sentinel on the hilltop of Montmartre.

The drizzle intensifies as they explore the city on foot. They pass interesting places, each street and corner revealing a new aspect of Paris. The I Love You Wall evokes a sense of romance shared by many around the world, while the Appartement des frères Vincent et Théo van Gogh resonates with the artistic history that permeates every corner of the city.

As they make their way up the stairs filled with people and trees that lead to Montmartre, they feel the energy of the city around them. The rain is now falling harder, creating an intimate and enveloping atmosphere. They finally reach the majestic Basilica of the Sacred Heart, an architectural jewel that seems to touch the sky itself.

Camille shares information about the Basilica, its impressive view, and the history that surrounds it. She describes how the Basilica of the Sacred Heart was built as a tribute to the nation's resilience after the turbulent times of the Franco-Prussian War and the Paris Commune. The resplendent white of the Basilica, she says, symbolizes the purity and hope that Parisians sought after the challenges they faced.

Luiz listens to her attentively, but something touches him deeply. He realizes that this journey is not just about exploring the city, but about sharing a special connection. He looks at Camille, feeling the intensity of the moment and the desire to express his feelings.

Before Camille has finished speaking, Luiz gently pulls her close and kisses her softly. This gesture is more than just a kiss, it's an expression of his feelings, a way of telling her how significant her presence is. Camille is surprised but soon surrenders to the moment, their lips meeting in a gesture that transcends words.

As the rain continues to fall, they pull away from the kiss, exchanging glances full of emotion. They turn to the view before them, Paris shrouded in a veil of rain that adds a special aura to the city.

Luiz and Camille's footsteps lead them back to the hotel, a sense of ecstasy filling the air as they cross the threshold.

Entering the suite, Camille soon comes across a captivating sight. A beautiful dark blue dress, with a fabric that is a perfect fusion of silk and linen, rests elegantly on a piece of furniture. Her eyes sparkle with admiration as she approaches Luiz's carefully chosen garment. Camille, her voice filled with genuine surprise and appreciation, speaks:

"Luiz, did you buy that? It's wonderful!"

Luiz smiles and replies:

"Yes, I wanted today to be special, so I brought you something that would match your beauty and elegance."

Camille's excitement grows when Luiz mentions a second gift that she will have to guess at dinner. She looks at him curiously and says:

"I can't wait to find out what the second present is..."

They then share a shower, the hot water enveloping them like an intimate embrace. Camille, with a playful smile, asks Luiz to wait for her in the Salon d'Été while she gets ready. He nods, his eyes fixed on her as she leaves the bathroom, a vision of grace.

Luiz goes downstairs to the Salon d'Été, where a cozy sofa awaits him. He settles in, his eyes getting lost in the beauty of the Grand Jardin stretching out before him.

Finally, the moment they had been waiting for arrives. Camille enters the salon, a picture of radiant beauty. The dark blue dress fits her perfectly, highlighting her natural elegance. Mancini is speechless for a moment, completely captivated by the vision unfolding before him. He whispers with his eyes fixed on her:

"Camille, you look stunning"

The surrounding people also turn to admire the scene, the impact of her presence being felt by all. It's not just the dress that makes her stunning, but the way she glows from the inside out. Camille smiles, her expression reflecting the joy and gratitude she feels.

Luiz and Camille's footsteps lead them out of the Ritz Hotel, a setting that has already become a vivid chapter in their history. They stop in front of the waiting cab, and Luiz instructs the driver to take them to an address near the River Seine, in the charming region of Auteuil.

As they arrive at their destination, their eyes fix on a majestic boat, its sails catching the glow of the Paris night. The sight is breathtaking, like something straight out of a movie. Luiz and Camille exchange a look of anticipation, anxiety mixing with the emotion that flows between them.

With anticipation growing, they enter the boat and are greeted by the maritime air that fills the room. Mancini approaches the waiter and informs him of their reservation. The waiter leads them gracefully through the boat, taking them to the top of the boat. They settle in, their eyes dancing amidst the beauty of the night that stretches out around them.

Luiz turns to Camille, a smile playing on his lips as his eyes meet hers:

"Camille, this is the second present."

He announces with a mixture of nervousness and excitement. Camille looks at him with surprise and gratitude, a mixture of feelings reflected in her clear eyes. She thanks Luiz, her words full of genuine appreciation, and says:

"Luiz, I'm loving every moment of this day with you. You really know how to make every moment special."

Camille shares another revelation, laughing as she mentions that she has never dined on a boat on the River Seine before. Her laughter infects the atmosphere around her. Luiz smiles in response, Camille's happiness turning into his own.

The succulent aroma of Argentinian beef cooking fills the air as Luiz and Camille enjoy a delicious meal. The rich flavors dance across their taste buds, a gastronomic experience that resembles a symphony of pleasure.

The night boat trip on the River Seine unfolds like a scene from a romantic movie. The city lit up at night unfolds before them, a magical scene that seems to have been designed by Paris itself. As the boat makes its way along the serene waters of the Seine, they witness the city coming to life in the darkness.

The Eiffel Tower sparkles like a jewel at night, its soft light casting mysterious shadows across the water. The Pont d' Iéna and the Alexandre III Bridge look like golden arches that connect their stories to the banks of the river. As the boat passes the Musée de l'Orangerie and the Musée d'Orsay, they feel the reverberation of the art that fills the city, an inspiration that floats in the air.

The Louvre Museum looms majestically, its historic walls full of secrets and wonders. The Pont des Arts, known for its love crossings, seems blessed by the presence of Louis and Camille. And when the boat passes the iconic Notre Dame, they feel a sense of reverence, as if they were witnessing the very soul of Paris.

The romantic passage during this three-hour ride is filled with moments that will become treasured memories. The two exchange smiles that share secrets and laughter that flows like a river of joy. They lean back together, their hands intertwined, as the city glides silently around them.

As the tour continues, they decide to have a limoncello drink with soda, ice, and lemon peel. The refreshing citrus flavor seems to be the perfect choice for the evening, a touch of freshness that complements the magical atmosphere around them. The sweet scent of lemon mingles with the gentle breeze that caresses their faces, creating a feeling of serenity and enchantment. The city lights reflected in the waters of the Seine create a spectacle of colors and shapes.

After the breathtaking walk, the couple returns to the cozy refuge of the hotel. Fresh memories of the Parisian night dance in their minds, like bright stars that refuse to fade. Every step they take seems to echo with the reverberation of the stories shared that day.

As they enter the suite, the atmosphere is charged with the feeling that something special has been experienced, something that transcends everyday experience. Luiz feels the need to preserve these ethereal moments, as if recording every detail in his heart wasn't enough. He picks up his journal and pen, allowing the words to flow like a serene river through his mind.

He writes down each place he visits, detailing the majesty of the Sacré-Coeur Basilica, the rich history of the Petit Palais, and the twinkling lights of the Seine boat trip. Every word he writes is an attempt to capture the essence of these ephemeral moments, to keep alive the feeling of being immersed in a Parisian tale.

But there is one part that he relates with a special touch of tenderness: Camille's beautiful company. He describes the sparkle in her eyes, the way she lit up every place with her presence. Every laugh shared, and every glance exchanged is encapsulated in the pages of the diary, becoming a precious treasure that he can revisit whenever he wants.

When Luiz finally closes the diary, a feeling of completeness envelops him. He puts the pen away and looks at the diary with a satisfied smile. With every word he writes, he feels he is leaving a mark on history, building a narrative that will be an indelible reminder of what they experienced together.

The suite becomes a sanctuary of calm and contemplation. Luiz lies down next to Camille, her presence like an anchor that connects him to the present moment. He watches her as she sleeps, amazed at the peace she transmits into his life.

And then, with the night enveloping them in its soft cloak, Luiz closes his eyes, his mind filled with images of the day he has just lived. He lets himself be carried away by the feeling of gratitude and happiness that floods his heart.

Colors Reflected in the Seine

After a few days, the charm of that night on the banks of the Seine remains, like a melodious song that refuses to leave Luiz and Camille's hearts. The bond between the Brazilian and the Frenchwoman seems to have grown, with each shared moment adding a new layer to the plot of romance they are weaving together.

Then comes Tuesday, a new chapter in their story that unfolds with the promise of exciting adventures. Mancini wakes up with a sense of anticipation in the air, an energy that seems to predict something special on the horizon. He decides to embark on a journey to an antique fair on the banks of the River Seine, an event that promises an enchanting encounter between the past and the present.

Luiz eats his breakfast, letting the rich, aromatic flavors awaken his senses. The hot cup in his hands is like a prelude to the day to come, an anticipation that builds in his chest. He gets up from the table, feeling the excitement pulsing through his veins, and decides to walk to the fair.

The sun shines high in the sky, its golden rays bathing the streets of Paris in radiant splendor. Every step he takes is a journey towards that encounter with the past, a moment that promises to unearth hidden treasures and ancient stories.

Arriving at the fair, Luiz is greeted by stalls full of old books and works of art, each object telling its own silent story. He strolls between the rows, his eyes captured by every detail, every piece waiting to be discovered.

The view of the Pont du Carrousel adds a touch of poetry to the atmosphere, the river flowing serenely under the bridge that is a silent witness to the stories unfolding on its banks. Luiz allows himself to get lost in the atmosphere, like a spectator at a show that is both nostalgic and ethereal.

In the middle of the antiques fair, Luiz lets his steps guide him, as if he were following the trails of history that dance in the air. His eyes find a stall that seems to overflow with secrets from the past. A crowd gathers around, eager to unearth fragments of times long lost. And then, among the treasures on display, he catches a glimpse of something that shines like a hidden gem.

It's an old leather object, a book or notebook, whose pages seem to have absorbed centuries of stories and dreams. The worn leather cover bears the marks of its journey through time, like the scars of a tireless traveler. Luiz is drawn to this mysterious artifact, a link that connects him to those who came before him.

He carefully takes the object in his hands, feeling the rough texture of the leather under his fingers. The yellowed pages whisper secrets that only time can understand. He examines every detail of that ancient piece. And it is at that moment that he decides that this object must be part of his own journey.

With determination, Luiz approaches the saleswoman at the stall, his eyes shining with the excitement of his discovery. He asks in a voice full of curiosity:

"How much does this object cost?

The writer points to the leather book, his hand almost touching the link between the past and the present.

The saleswoman at the stall picks it up. She examines the label carefully, as if reading the words that history has inscribed on the heart of that object, and then speaks:

"About 15 euros."

Luiz doesn't hesitate. He feels the connection that object represents, the link with those who came before him and the stories he has yet to discover. With a decisive gesture, he takes out his wallet and pays the seller the sum of 15 euros, becoming an investment in a piece of shared history.

So, after acquiring the enigmatic leather object, Luiz lets himself be carried away by an inexplicable impulse and begins to wander along the banks of the River Seine. The waters scatter the sunlight with an almost unreal glow, as if the river were also aware of the aura of mystery that surrounds it. The gentle breeze caresses his face, while his slow, purposeful strides seem guided by destiny.

With the leather object in his hands, Luiz feels the pulse of history beating in his fingers. Curiosity consumes him as he decides to explore the contents of those old pages. He opens the book with an irreverent touch, as if he were about to unveil a long-kept secret.

The sun casts golden rays over the pages, illuminating the characters that form an unknown tale. And then, as your eyes scan the first few lines, something extraordinary begins to happen. Daylight seems to melt into a profusion of colors, like brushstrokes in an impressionist painting. The world around him dissolves, and the figures walking along the riverbank become blurs of color as if they were part of a living canvas.

Luiz feels a sense of vertigo, as if he had entered a portal to another dimension. His heart races as he continues to read, absorbing the words that now flow like a river of emotions. Each line is like a stroke of paint that brings the narrative to life, each word is a brushstroke that forms an image in his mind.

And then, amid this whirlwind of colors and sensations, Luiz comes across something that takes his breath away. The words that fill the pages are not just those of an unknown author, but the thoughts, dreams, and memories of Claude Monet, one of the greatest impressionist painters who ever lived.

The revelation hits him like a thunderbolt, a shock of admiration and bewilderment. He reads attentively, his eyes moving along the lines that capture the artist's voice, the essence of his creative mind. The date on the first page is 1869, and the words tell of Monet's move to Paris, a crucial moment in his artistic journey.

While reading, Luiz finds himself immersed in that impressionist aura, almost as if Monet's brushstrokes had covered the world around him. The sun's rays dance across the pages of the diary, forming a choreography of colors and sensations that echo the artist's unique vision. It's as if Luiz is living one of the landscapes that Monet so skillfully transposed onto canvas, a vision that transcends time.

Suddenly, a voice breaks through Luiz's braid of thoughts, like a surprise note in a symphony:

"So you're reading my life... I should have disappeared with that diary a long time ago."

The words are full of surprise and a touch of bitterness, as if the story contained in the pages of the diary was a secret that should have been kept more carefully.

Luiz's eyes lift from the diary and meet the gaze of a man who seems to have emerged from one of Monet's paintings. Claude Monet's long beard *flows like a river of time, his bright, deep eyes reflecting centuries of creativity and experience. The presence of the artist in front of him is almost as if a page from the past has come to life.*

Luiz's disbelief is palpable as if he were facing a being that transcends reality. The words come out of his trembling lips, almost stammering:

"Are you Claude Monet?!"

The question hangs in the air, like an empty canvas about to be filled with the artist's colors. Monet smiles, a serene expression that seems to carry all the weight of time. He nods, confirming the identity that transcends the centuries, and speaks:

"Don't be alarmed, my friend. And what is your name?"

Luiz replies:

"Luiz Mancini"

Mancini extends his hand, shaking hands with the artist who now stands before him, a meeting of two worlds separated by decades, but united by a passion for art and a curiosity that transcends the ages.
Luiz and Monet's hands meet, a grip that crosses the barriers of time. In this way, Monet speaks with an affable smile, his words resonating in the present, but carrying with them the colors of a distant past:

"You were reading about my move to Paris," he says, his voice full of warmth and nostalgia. "It was a wonderful time."

Monet's words seem to dance in the air, carrying with them the memories of a young man in love with art and the city that welcomed him.

Then, as if time itself were writhing, a flashback appears in front of the two men. Luiz feels transported to a period that is not his own, but which is now unfolding before his eyes like a magical story. Monet returns to the Paris of 1859 and 1860, a Paris that was bubbling with the creative energy of the Barbizon School.

Luiz is a silent spectator of this journey through time, watching the young Monet absorb the influence of the paintings of Charles Daubigny and Constant Troyon. The air is full of promise and enthusiasm as if the very spirit of Paris were blowing in his sails. Monet seems an ethereal figure, a manifestation of the passion for art, exploring the streets and parks with eager eyes and hands ready to capture the essence of life on his canvases.

The parks become Monet's refuge, a place where he seeks harmony between nature and art. Luiz watches with admiration as the young painter approaches the trees, the rivers, and the colors that dance in the breeze. It's as if the very essence of Impressionism is being transmitted through Monet's eyes and brushes.

Every sketch, every brushstroke, and every stroke of color resonates as an expression of Monet's soul. Luiz can almost feel the artist's heart beating in tune with the city that inspired him.

The flashback of Monet's life unfolds before Mancini's eyes like a series of living paintings, each scene full of color and vivid emotion. It's as if the past is coming to life, inviting Luiz to witness the artist's inspiring journey. He finds himself immersed in this magical spectacle, observing the courageous choices and connections that shaped Monet's career.

Despite his family's insistence, Monet refused to follow the conventional, traditional path. The School of Fine Arts may have clamored for his presence, but Monet chose to follow a different path, one that led him to explore the broad and limitless horizons of outdoor art. It's as if the city of Paris became Monet's own studio, a stage where he joined other visionaries.

Monet, as a central character in this plot, reveals chapters that echo the colors and textures of his life. Luiz watches as Monet goes on to work at the Swiss Academy, his brushes creating images that portray the world around him. But life doesn't always follow a straight path, and Monet is called up to serve in the army in Algeria. Luiz feels the tension and intrigue of this turning point in history, a forced pause in his artistic career that is like an interrupted color palette.

After his service in the army, Monet resumes his path in art, revealing details of his relentless pursuit of improvement. He shares with Luiz his studies with Charles Gleyer in Paris, where Monet's paths crossed with other art luminaries such as Camille Pissarro and Gustave Courbet. Together, they unveiled the possibilities of quick brushstrokes and ephemeral light, a technique that would redefine art and become known as Impressionism. Luiz observes how Monet and his fellow painters were like alchemists, transforming paint and canvas into glimpses of reality transfigured by light and emotion.

However, Monet's journey is not a straight line to success. Luiz contemplates the difficulties and challenges that are part of the artist's path. Nomadic life, marked by comings and goings, moments of uncertainty and overcoming, emerges as an underlying theme in this account. Monet shares his struggles, his struggles for recognition and sustenance, and the dark colors that contrast with the vibrant brushstrokes of light in his works.

In the twilight of the narrative, Claude Monet and Luiz share a moment of farewell in the magical setting of the past. The artist turns his gaze gently toward Mancini, his face illuminated by the colors of the story he has just shared. Monet's words carry the weight of a reality that transcends time, and he says to Luiz:

"It's very late now, Luiz. I think we'd better go back."

Mancini, touched by the depth of this experience, silently agrees with the painter. He then closes the diary with reverence, but when the pages come together, the magic that surrounds the past seems to fade. The reality around him reaffirms its presence, the people resuming their forms and the city regaining its familiarity. However, a figure still remains in front of Luiz, a vision of Monet that persists as a trace of that unusual encounter.

The impressionist artist, now a specter of a bygone era, speaks once more:

"See you later, Luiz. We can see each other and talk any time you open my diary, because I'll always be there."

Luiz replies:

"Sure, we'll see each other again! See you, buddy."

And so the heartfelt goodbye, the feeling of a special connection warming his heart. Monet gradually disappears, like a dream that dissipates at dawn.

The darkness of the night envelops Luiz, but he finds himself stunned as he looks at the clock. Time seems to have distorted, an illusion unfolding before his eyes. What seemed like mere minutes in that alternative reality now *translates into hours in the real world. Luiz is perplexed by the ephemeral nature of time and the mysterious connection he has experienced.*

Between the lines of the present and the past

Late at night in Paris, Luiz takes the initiative to call Camille. He invites her to meet him in a charming bistro near the Musée Maillol, where they can share the latest twists and turns in their lives. Camille readily accepts and meets Luiz, taking a seat at a table that seems to have been reserved especially for them. The atmosphere is full of anticipation and curiosity.

As Camille settles in, Luiz recounts the extraordinary experience he had while immersing himself in the pages of Claude Monet's diary. He speaks with a mixture of excitement and bewilderment, confessing to Camille that he feels as if he is losing his sanity. The expression on his face is a mixture of admiration and unease, as if he were trying to reconcile the inexplicable with tangible reality.

With a tone of caution, Luiz advises Camille not to open the diary immediately. He explains that the dimension of that alternative reality is profoundly distorted, with time unfolding in an unpredictable way. He tries to convey the complexity of the situation, a narrative that seems to come from the pages of a science fiction novel.

Camille looks at the leather object resting on the table, its worn and aged cover suggesting a long and rich history. She examines the diary with curiosity, while Luiz anxiously awaits her reaction. She comments on the condition of the leather and remarks that it seems to have seen the passing of many years, almost as if it had witnessed the passage of time.

The conversation takes a new turn when Camille shares details of her own day. She mentions that she is working in marketing for a renowned French perfume company, an activity that echoes the elegance and sophistication of the city in which they live. With a graceful gesture, she takes a sample of perfume out of her bag and applies a light spray to her skin. She turns to Luiz, smiling endearingly, and asks:

"Do you like the smell?"

Luiz tilts his head slightly and closes his eyes for a moment, inhaling the soft scent that fills the air. He describes the perfume as a symphony of lavender with subtle hints of orange peel. And he says it smells good. Camille laughs softly and confirms that Luiz's description is very close to what the perfume represents.

The evening unfolds, and as dinner draws to a close, they both get up from the bistro table with a feeling of fullness. The walk back to the hotel is punctuated by soft laughter and intimate conversations, which echo like soft musical notes in the nocturnal atmosphere of Paris.

Arriving at the cozy hotel, Luiz wastes no time and takes out his notebook. He begins to record every detail, every emotion, and every word that flows from his mind like a river of thoughts. The pen glides across the paper, capturing the magic of the day and the extraordinary interaction with Monet. As the words accumulate on the paper, Luiz feels a sense of catharsis, as if he were eternalizing that unique experience.

However, when he finally decides to rest next to Camille, he notices that her eyes are already closed in a peaceful sleep. Mancini watches her for a moment, enchanted by the serenity that emanates from her even in repose. He lies down next to her, but as Camille sinks into the depths of sleep, Luiz finds his mind restless.

In the darkness of the bedroom, he finds himself plunged into a sea of turbulent thoughts. The images of his encounter with Monet intertwine with his own longings and goals in life. He reflects on his journey so far, the choices he has made, and the ambitions that have driven him. The silent city outside the windows seems to reflect his own inner questioning.

Hours pass, and the ticking of the clock seems to echo in his mind. The moon travels across the night sky, casting shadows that dance across the bedroom walls. Finally, after a night of introspection and self-evaluation, Luiz feels that his reflections have found some sort of resolution. A serenity takes over his being as if he had found a glimmer of clarity in the midst of confusion.

After a few days, Luiz felt an inner call and a sense of restlessness that led him to seek out Claude Monet's presence once again. With firm determination, he heads for the Luxembourg Gardens, as if following an invisible thread that connects him to this unique reality. He finds a quiet spot near a fountain, where the gentle murmur of the water seems to be the perfect soundtrack for the imminent encounter.

Sitting on a chair, Mancini holds Monet's diary with reverence. The pages of this magical object are a passage into a dimension that defies the boundaries of time. He opens the diary and, as he does so, he feels as if he is crossing an invisible portal. The environment around him begins to take on a soft, diffuse tone, as if the colors were blending in a subtle way, creating a scene that reflects Monet's impressionist aesthetic.

In front of him, Monet appears like a specter of history, a man whose essence transcends the barriers of time. The painter's voice resonates softly:

"So you've come, friend, I've been waiting for you."

Luiz stands up, feeling a mixture of excitement and reverence. He walks alongside Monet, and the park seems transformed as if it had been immersed in a moving canvas.

As they walk, Monet breaks the silence with a gentle question about Luiz's life. Luiz, for his part, shares his uncertainties and questions, confessing the duality he experiences between being a writer and the possibility of taking over the family business. The artist, with his unique wisdom, responds in a serene voice, encouraging him to follow his dreams and passion:

"We should always follow our dreams."

Luiz nods but doesn't hide his internal battle. He reveals that being a writer is a quest that often hurts, a journey full of challenges and questions. The artist listens attentively, his presence radiating empathy and understanding. He offers words of encouragement, like a spiritual guide who knows the complexities of the human heart.

The conversation between the two continues as they walk through the garden, among diffuse colors and deep reflections. Luiz feels that he is sharing not only his concerns but also his deepest yearnings as if the painter could see beyond words and understand the nuances of his soul. Then the artist looks at Luiz with a friendly gaze and says:

"Remember, my friend, the journey of life is like a painting in constant evolution."

Claude Monet, with the wisdom that only experience can provide, shares with Luiz the concrete example that every dream requires sacrifices and a continuous process of evolution. The narrative of the flashbacks unfolds before them, revealing vivid details of the artist's life. Time seems to be a fluid stream, allowing both of them to observe key moments that shaped the impressionist artist's journey.

Luiz's eyes fixate on the part of Monet's life in 1863, a crucial year. The painter, helped by his friend and the inner fire that drove him, rents a modest studio in Paris. With every brushstroke and drop of paint, he brought to life the visions that inhabited his mind. Perseverance is his muse, and he is undeterred by the difficulties that stand in his way.

In the same year, Monet's name was entered in the official Paris Painting Salon with notable works such as "Estuary of the Seine" and "Bridge over Hève at the Leak". These works capture the essence of nature in evolution, a reflection of the constant change that also permeates an artist's life. Monet not only paints the landscape but also the transformation of the human soul.

The narrative flow continues, and the journey through time continues. In 1864, Monet once again made his mark at the Paris Salon with works such as "Camille" or "The Green Dress", where the painter's talent was praised by the critics and rewarded with a prize. "Camille" depicts Monet's future wife, Camille Doncieux, in a portrait that transcends time and the person portrayed. The canvas breathes life and emotion as if capturing an eternal moment.

In 1867, the artist faced challenges and rejection at the Paris Salon when he tried to enter his work "Women in the Garden". Determined to overcome the obstacles, he adapted his approach, building a trench to paint the upper part of the canvas. He persevered, even in the face of adversity, and his resilient spirit is reflected in his art.

The year 1868 marked a period of financial difficulty for Monet. A painting of his entered the Paris Salon, "Ship Leaving Le Havre Quay", was met with negative reviews. However, the artist remained undeterred and, that same year, his work "Le Havre Pier" was recognized with a silver medal at the International Maritime Exhibition in Le Havre. Once again, Monet faces life's challenging events with the courage of a true creator and dreamer.

The atmosphere is magical and intense as the Frenchman shares another vibrant chapter of his life with Luiz. The artist's words opens a window onto the summer of 1869, when the colors of the River Seine and the reflections of the golden sun inspired a movement that would transcend generations: Impressionism.

With a narrative full of vivid details, Monet takes Luiz on a journey back in time to the picturesque seaside resort of Bougival, a refuge on the left bank of the River Seine. This is where Monet and Auguste Renoir, his partner in artistic vision, settled. Together, they created a series of canvases that would become the first examples of the movement that would mark the history of art.

Luiz's eyes are drawn to the vision of the canvases in his mind as if he were witnessing the creation himself. Nature takes shape in the skilled hands of the artists, and the sun kisses the water of the river, reflecting a spectacle of light and color. The broad, bold brushstrokes challenge the academic traditions of the time, opening up space for the creative freedom that characterizes Impressionism.

Through Monet's words, Luiz follows the journey of colors, shapes, and emotions, immersed in the wonder of artistic discovery. The energy that permeates each stroke is palpable, and the fusion between nature and the artist's soul creates a timeless bond.

And then, like a final jewel in a necklace of history, Monet reveals the creation of the canvas "Bathers of Grenouillière". Luiz glimpses the picturesque scene, almost as if he were at the water's edge watching the bathers plunge into the serenity of the river. Monet's touch on the canvas brings out not only the scenery but also the subtle emotions of the moment, a unique signature that shaped the course of the Impressionist movement.

Under the mixture of blue colors in the sky, the conversation between Luiz and Monet deepens, like a stream of thoughts shared in the present. Claude Monet, with a penetrating gaze, directs his attention to Luiz and asks a question loaded with meaning:

"Do you love someone, my friend? And what do you think about love?"

The writer, looking at Monet with a mixture of reflection and sincerity, answered with conviction:

"Yes, I love someone. I love Camille."

He pauses, searching for the words that reflect his perceptions of love, and then speaks:

"Love is like a constant evolution, a foundation that blends and transforms over time. It's a feeling that drives us, that makes us see the beauty in every detail of life."

Luiz's words echo in the air, like notes of a sincere melody that resonates between their souls. The painter, with a serene smile, nods in approval, understanding the depth of Luiz's words and speaks:

"Love is, in fact, a journey of constant discovery."

As Luiz's words opened a door to the past, a new flashback emerges from the shadows of memory. The two meet in a small church, immersed in the solemn atmosphere of a wedding. The name "Camille" resonates, as Monet has found love on more than one occasion. The woman standing next to him, also called Camille, is the central figure in this love scene eternalized by time.

The scene comes to life before Luiz's eyes. The exchange of glances between Monet and his beloved Camille is so profound that it seems to transcend words. They share a love that goes beyond convention, shaping the very essence of their souls. Luiz witnesses the birth of this union, a marriage that blossomed after the birth of their first child.

Monet's voice resonates again, filling the space between them with palpable emotion:

"This is the best thing I've ever done in my life," he says, with a twinkle in his eyes that reveals the depth of his emotions. "I gave my heart and soul to my beloved. It was the greatest decision I've ever made."

Luiz feels the value of Monet's words reverberate in his own understanding of love. He understands that love is not just a feeling, but a conscious choice, a complete surrender of oneself to another person.

The writer, feeling the hunger rising, decides to pause momentarily. He looks at Claude, who remains by his side and announces his intention to satisfy his hunger. He gently closes the impressionist painter's diary, and the world around him returns to its everyday reality, although the painter is still there, like a faint presence that continues to accompany him.

Monet, with his serene gaze and affable smile, nods and says:

"Come on, my friend, I'll join you for your afternoon snack."

In this way, Luiz crosses the park, under the shelter of the trees that cast dancing shadows over the path. He explores his surroundings until he finds a cozy snack bar near L'Acteur Grec. The scent of delicious delicacies floats in the air, inviting him in. He enters the place, a picturesque haven that seems to have been taken straight out of an impressionist painting.

In front of the counter, Luiz places his order: a croissant, which shines golden and tempting, and a generous plate of salami and cheese, enriched by the presence of a raspberry jam, following Monet's wise advice. The delicacy becomes a tribute to the words and knowledge shared by that timeless artist.

While Luiz enjoys the bittersweetness of the raspberry jam combined with the intensity of the flavors of the salami and cheese, Monet, with a smile, shares his own affection for the dish:

"Ah, that bittersweet taste is a real masterpiece, isn't it? Life is like that too, full of contrasts that make it unique and beautiful."

Mancini smiles, satisfied not only with the snack he has selected but also with the enriching dialog he shares with the painter.

After savoring every bite of his snack, Luiz heads towards the area known as Harde de cerfs écoutant le rapproché, a quiet nook in the park. The green grass stretches gently in the dazzling sunlight, creating a serene and welcoming setting. Luiz settles down on the grass next to the sculpture, and next to him, the figure of the impressionist Monet appears again, like a link between the times.

The diary is opened once again, like a window into a past that echoes in the present. Luiz's curiosity is piqued, and he searches for the words that will bring to life the questions that reside in his mind. With a quiet voice, he asks Monet about the work "Red Cloak", wanting to understand the motivation behind that painting that marked the artist's memory.

The painter, with his deep, expressive gaze, inclines his head in consideration and speaks:

"Ah, 'Red Cloak'," he murmurs as if reliving a special moment. "It was during the harsh winters that I found the inspiration for this painting. The city was covered in snow, and the sunlight reflected on the landscape created a unique spectacle of tones and shadows."

He draws an invisible image in the air, outlining the contours of the scene with gentle hand movements, and speaks to Luiz:

"I created 'Red Cloak' in the small village of Giverny, where the houses hid under blankets of snow and the fields displayed a delicate palette of whites and grays."

Monet stares into the distance for a moment, as if reliving those moments of creation:

"What motivated me, Luiz, was the incessant quest to capture the fleeting atmosphere, the light that danced over the landscape. The red cover, a vibrant touch of color amid the winter landscape, represented the vivacity of life, even in the coldest seasons."

He smiles as if he could feel the same emotion of those bygone days. So Mancini continues through the enchanting landscape of his transformed reality, where the colors blend together like the strokes of an impressionist painting. His steps take him to the Fontaine des Quatre-Parties-du-Monde, an imposing water fountain that seems to emerge from the very impressionist scene that surrounds it. Next to Monet, they stop to admire the aquatic spectacle unfolding before them.

Claude Monet, with his attentive gaze, shares curiosities about the fountain, bringing to life the stories hidden behind those architectural elements. He tells them that the four bronze female figures represent the four corners of the world. Luiz listens to each word like a treasure, feeling transported not only to the era but to the stories that make up every detail of that landscape.

With a gentle gesture, the writer opens the painter's diary again, exploring the same year that Claude got married. The words written there reveal a remarkable chapter in the painter's life: the start of the Franco-Prussian War. The lines of the diary tell how the artist's family was forced to seek refuge in London, fleeing the turbulence of the war. Luiz's eyes follow the words as he feels the gravity of that historic moment echoing in his consciousness.

Monet shares his experience with a tone of introspection. He tells Luiz about returning to France after the war, his father no longer present. The shadows of his hometown, Le Havre, didn't attract him as before. In search of a new horizon, the artist chose Argenteuil as his refuge. In this city, he found a haven of inspiration and tranquility, a place where nature and art could flourish in harmony.

Suddenly, as if the veil of time were opening, the scene in front of them is transformed to reveal Argenteuil, an emblematic place in Claude Monet's journey. The atmosphere reappears with vitality, and Luiz finds himself witnessing a moment in the Impressionist's life.

In the streets of Argenteuil, friendship and a passion for art united Monet and his fellow Impressionists. The names of Édouard Manet, Pierre-Auguste Renoir, and Alfred Sisley emerge as figures who shared the same passions and innovative visions. Luiz is caught up in this web of relationships and collaborations, feeling the effervescent atmosphere that permeates the artists' conversations and canvases.

The city of Argenteuil becomes a scene of inspiration, where the River Seine meanders, mirroring the sky and the landscapes that stretch out before the attentive eyes of Monet and his friends. Luiz witnesses how nature became a crucial ally, providing the raw material for his iconic works. He is transported to a world where every brushstroke is an attempt to capture the ever-changing light and colors.

Monet shares with Luiz his deep affection for painting by the river. The image of small sailing boats passing along the Seine materializes, filling the scene with picturesque charm.

In this way, Mancini can almost feel the gentle breeze and the murmur of the water, as if the scene itself were inviting him to become part of that creative experience. The dialog between Monet and Luiz blends in with the environment, creating a sense of complete immersion in the history of art and the painter's life.

The city of Argenteuil, which seemed to have come to life in impressionist colors, gradually dissipates, returning to the serene landscape of the park. Luiz closes the diary with a mixture of reverence and gratitude, and his reality regains its everyday shape. However, Monet remains in front of him, a presence that transcends time and space.

With a look full of understanding, Monet suggests to Luiz that, before returning to the hotel, he should pay a visit to Montparnasse Cemetery. Luiz welcomes the suggestion and prepares to leave, feeling a new energy pulsating inside him. The impressionist painter's advice seems to be an invitation to a profound experience, perhaps a reflection on the meaning of life or a conclusion to their unique encounter.

On the way to the cemetery, Claude breaks the silence and asks Luiz about his recent activities. With a smile, he replies:

"I'm looking for something innovative, something that transcends the pages and reaches people's core. He expresses his desire to tell authentic stories, stories that touch readers' souls, just as impressionist art touched his own heart."

The artist listens attentively as if he can sense the passion that drives the young writer. He understands the essence of what Luiz wants to create, as he himself has always sought to convey emotions and ephemeral moments through his canvases. The dialog between the two becomes an enriching exchange of ideas, where art and writing intertwine in a moment of deep connection. Monet then speaks:

"It takes courage to follow your artistic vision, to dare to innovate and create something that is true to you. Authenticity is what makes art touch people's hearts."

Arriving at Montparnasse Cemetery, you can feel the quiet, contemplative atmosphere of the place. The old gravestones tell silent stories, and the atmosphere seems charged with reflections on the ephemerality of life and the eternity that lies beyond it. Claude Monet, standing next to Luiz, seems to be immersed in deep thoughts as they walk through the corridors between the graves and says:

"It's amazing how life and death intertwine in this place, how each tombstone tells a unique story that blends into the fabric of time."

Mancini listens attentively to the painter's words as he walks through the cemetery. Monet goes on to talk about his own experiences and views on life and death. He mentions how the loss of loved ones led him to contemplate the ephemeral nature of human life, and how this inspired him to create art that captured fleeting moments:

"As we lose those we love, we are reminded of the fragility of existence. But we can also find comfort in the idea that there is something greater beyond what we can see. I believe that life is a test, a process of evolution towards something greater, something that transcends the mortal."

But Luiz shares his doubts about the meaning of life and death, questioning the cycle of rising from the dust and returning to it. The painter looks at him with wise eyes and says:

"My writer friend, I believe the answer lies in embracing the mystery and trusting the process. Life is like a journey, and what matters is the search for truth, for a connection with something greater. You have dreams and passions for a reason, they are the thread that connects us to something divine, to an eternal love that permeates everything. Take a chance on your dream, don't give up, because even in uncertainty, there is beauty and purpose."

As the sun begins to set and the shadows lengthen across the cemetery, Luiz feels a sense of clarity and inspiration. He looks at the gravestones and realizes that, despite the finitude of life, there is a power that transcends human understanding.

With evening approaching, the walk through the cemetery comes to an end. Although the atmosphere may seem funereal at first glance, it's surprising to see the number of tourists strolling around, exploring one of the city's unique sights. The gardens and corridors, now illuminated by the soft lights of the lamps, reveal a peaceful and respectful aura.

While Luiz and Monet prepare to leave the cemetery, the writer bids farewell to the painter with a feeling of gratitude. Monet fades from his sight as if returning to the fabric of time that brought them together for a brief moment. As Luiz walks through the Parisian streets, the night sky begins to come alive. Stars share the firmament, inviting him to reflect on everything he has witnessed throughout the day.

Dialogues Under the Shade of Flowers

At the hotel, Luiz shares with Camille the extraordinary experiences he had with Monet, describing in detail the paintings he witnessed being created by the impressionist artist. As his words flow, Camille listens attentively, but a shadow of skepticism seems to hang over her eyes. Luiz's stories are so engaging, so full of wonder, that Camille begins to wonder if it's all just the fruit of an exceptionally vivid imagination.

Cautiously, she doesn't want to doubt Luiz's words, but the idea of encounters with a 19th-century painter and the experience of witnessing moments that transcend the barriers of time and reality are concepts that defy common logic and understanding. So, as she listens, her mind oscillates between accepting Luiz's magical narrative and seeking a more rational explanation.

Faced with Camille's skepticism, Mancini, with kindness and understanding, proposes a solution to dispel her doubts. He suggests that, before they go to sleep, she accompany him the next day to experience these extraordinary events for herself. This suggestion could be the key to unraveling the mystery surrounding these unlikely encounters and give Camille the opportunity to experience a reality that defies the limits of time and imagination.

With the promise of a new day, the silence of the night envelops the couple. As the couple settle under the sheets, Paris rests under a starry sky, serene and magical. The encounter with Monet not only added a touch of the surreal to their routine but also brought up an avalanche of emotions and questions. Now, united by a desire to explore the unexplored, they are preparing to *embark on yet another extraordinary journey in search of answers and, perhaps, the truth behind their encounters with the artist of yesteryear.*

After sharing a morning coffee in the charming garden of the Ritz Hotel, Luiz feels a new inspiration pulsing within him. Under the clear, sunny sky, he turns to Camille with a look of enthusiasm and proposes an intriguing idea. The words flow from Luiz's lips:

"Camille, it's a wonderful day, with a clear, bright sky. What if, just for a moment, we abandoned our routines and ventured into a place that only existed on the pages of books and in our most vivid dreams?"

The suggestion hung in the air, full of curiosity and longing. Listening to Luiz's words, she replies:

"Absolutely," she replies, with a mixture of enthusiasm and curiosity. "If there's an opportunity to dive into a reality that defies the boundaries of imagination and see with my own eyes what you tell me. Why shouldn't we take it?"

So, under the bright morning sun, Luiz and Camille set off on a new discovery. Leaving behind the cozy walls of the Hotel Ritz, they head for the train station with a mixture of excitement and anticipation. The station at Gare de l'Est Paris, where they set off for Giverny, is an architectural marvel that has witnessed countless departures and arrivals over the years. The platforms stretch out under the blue sky, an invitation to embark on a journey that promises to transcend time and reality.

With tickets in hand, the two exchange smiles full of anticipation. Their luggage is carefully packed, while they wait for the train signal that will take them to Monet's house. The gentle wind caresses their skin, bringing with it the scent of the city as it awakens to another day of life.

Finally, the train approaches, and they board with a sense of excitement that seems to echo in the beating of their hearts. The cozy seats welcome them, offering a place to sit while the Paris landscape glides past the window.

In the train cabin, Luiz and Camille are transported to a world that unfolds in front of their windows. As the locomotive moves forward, they surrender to the ever-changing landscape, as if they were watching a movie chronicling the journey from Paris to Giverny. With each new season, a new scene unfolds, painted in the vibrant colors of spring.

The journey of about an hour and fifteen minutes reveals a true visual spectacle. First, they glimpse Nanterre, a fleeting glimpse between the trees that marks the beginning of the journey. Memories of Argenteuil echo in Luiz's mind as the train moves forward at a steady, reassuring pace.

Montesson appears, bringing with him a serene view of the Dominican forest of Saint-Germain. The trees display an exuberant green as if they were preparing to greet the travelers with their majestic natural beauty. Passing through Saint-Germain-en-Laye is a moment of contemplation, where historic buildings and picturesque scenery blend in harmony.

Poissy presents itself with its personality, with streams meandering through a region that seems timeless. The old buildings tell stories of centuries gone by, while the train continues its journey along the majestic River Seine. The waters reflect the sky, creating a lyrical image that could well have been taken from a canvas.

By the time the train approaches Mantes-la-Jolie, the details become clearer. The outlines of the buildings and landscapes are drawn in vivid, defined colors, as if Monet himself were applying his magic brushes to the scene. Rolleboise offers a serene and tranquil view, captured in a fleeting instant that remains imprinted in the memory.

And then, with a majestic crossing, the River Seine is crossed and Giverny is finally revealed. The long-awaited destination where Monet brought his masterpieces to life is within reach. The station in Giverny welcomes Louis and Camille as if they were entering a new world. The train journey, full of captivating sights, is now a memory, a trail left behind as they prepare to explore what Giverny has to offer.

Deciding to explore a little further before arriving at Monet's house, Luiz and Camille disembark in Giverny and begin to unravel the charms of this picturesque village. A scene that seems to have been painted by Claude comes to life in front of them, and the bucolic and serene atmosphere envelops them as if they were entering a living painting.

Their steps take them to the Vignes de Giverny, where the production of wines and grape juices seems to be a reverence to the generous nature that surrounds the village. The landscape of the vineyards adds a touch of rusticity to Giverny, creating a perfect balance between the artistic and the earthy.

Giverny's Sainte-Radegonde Church turns out to be a beautiful building, a monument that carries with it the history and faith of the town. Camille gazes at the church as if its presence were a tribute to the past that intertwines with the present. The silence of the place seems to resonate with the tranquility and devotion of those who sought refuge there.

While exploring the streets of Giverny, Luiz and Camille come across art galleries where local artists exhibit their creations inspired by the same scenery that captivated the Impressionist movement. Luiz's gaze is fixed on the colors, shapes, and expressions that make up this artistic world that seems so connected to the soul of the town.

Luiz's astute observation does not overlook the fact that the region is a true symphony of nature. The trees that stand like guardians, and the landscapes that blend together in harmony, all contribute to a beauty that is both tranquil and magnificent.

Still walking through picturesque Giverny, Luiz and Camille come across the Musée des Impressionnismes Giverny, a cultural gem that fits in perfectly with the town's artistic scene. An invitation to immerse themselves in the world of Impressionism, the museum arouses the curiosity of the two lovers. Camille looks at Luiz and proposes the idea of going inside, perhaps in search of a deeper connection with the atmosphere that surrounded Impressionism. An affirmative nod from Luiz is enough to seal the decision.

Entering the museum, Luiz feels a sense of anticipation, as if every step brings him closer to something extraordinary. He shares his intuition with Camille, advising her to prepare herself for a unique, almost magical experience. She, still maintaining a cautious reserve, watches Luiz open Monet's old diary, the link between the present and the past.

As they progress through the Musée des Impressionnismes, something out of the ordinary happens. The atmosphere is transformed, every corner and detail radiating an impressionist aura. The colors come alive, the brushstrokes seem to float in the atmosphere, and the canvases seem to breathe in harmony. Camille, perplexed and enchanted, witnesses the reality around *her metamorphose into a living painting as if the painter had brushed the atmosphere itself.*

Faced with this surreal scene, Luiz notices the look of astonishment in Camille's eyes. He sees the opportunity to share with her something that until then only he had experienced. Camille sees before her the iconic figure of Claude Monet. The painter, like an enchanting mirage, seems to materialize from the very paint and canvas that he so skillfully handled.

Mancini, for his part, observes the expression of admiration and surprise on Camille's face. He feels gratified to be able to share this moment, this connection between past and present, between dream and reality.

Monet looks at Luiz with a mixture of curiosity and approval, her voice echoing calmly:

"So this is your beloved?"

He extends his hand in a friendly gesture and greets Camille, who seems slightly stunned by the iconic figure. She, still somewhat incredulous, lets out her words with a slight tremor:

"You could say that." The surprise in her eyes is palpable, and she adds, "I can't believe it's you in front of me."

The artist doesn't hold back a gentle smile, an expression that reflects years of experience, but also a certain glow of recognition. He begins to walk alongside the couple as if to acknowledge their presence in the museum. In the setting that looks like a painting coming to life, Monet shares stories and anecdotes about his works, recreating the atmosphere in which each brushstroke was applied.

In addition, while looking at the Impressionist paintings of his colleagues from the movement there, Monet turns to the two visitors with a look of regret. His words resonate with a mixture of nostalgia and pain:

"Renoir, Bazille, and I faced the painful rejection of our paintings by the Paris Salon, a rejection that could almost be touched, such was the weight of our emotions."

The painter shares with Luiz the deep scars that this rejection left on his soul. The pain of rejection, and the feeling that his art was not recognized as it deserved, all of this echoes through the decades, becoming a reminder of the complexities of the creative quest and the artist's journey.

But what could have been the end for many artists became the starting point for Claude and his fellow Impressionists. They choose not to crumble in the face of adversity, choosing instead to tread an unexplored path. The courage that permeates their actions is palpable, and Luiz finds himself immersed in this moment of determination and vision.

The painter tells the story of the first Impressionist exhibition with passion as if he were recounting a transcendental event. Mancini and Camille as witnesses to these artists, united by their bold vision and tireless determination, decided to challenge the established norms and create a movement that would shake the foundations of art. The Impressionist revolution was about to begin.

Monet and his colleagues' journey is not just about painting, but also about yearning for freedom and authenticity. They dared to be different, they sought beauty in the ephemeral light and vibrant colors of everyday life. Each stroke of the brush, each quick, fluid brushstroke, is like an affirmation of their unique vision.

The three walk through the museum, immersed in a sea of colors and brushstrokes that echo the voices of innovative artists. As they explore the museum's collection, their visions unfold in front of a spectacle of creativity. The walls are filled with canvases that capture the essence of the Impressionist movement. Claude then speaks:

"Look at Renoir's 'Woman with an Umbrella'."

He points to a painting depicting an elegantly dressed woman walking with an umbrella in a very flowery garden. The bright colors and quick brushstrokes give the work a sense of movement and life as if the woman were about to take another step.

Next, they approach a canvas showing a bed of lilies in a serene lake. Monet smiles fondly as he looks at the work:

"My lilies."

The painter reveals his deep connection with nature and his search for the representation of light and the ever-changing atmosphere.

Luiz observes a painting that catches his eye and says:

"That painting of Pissarro's 'Avenida de los Campos Elíseos' is beautiful!"

It shows a busy street with people and carriages. The bright colors and vivid contrasts give the painting a vibrant energy as if the chaos of urban life were captured in a single scene.

In the corner of the museum, they find a series of self-portraits by various Impressionist artists, each reflecting their unique personalities and approaches to art. Monet explains that these self-portraits are not only a reflection of how the artists see themselves, but also a representation of the evolution of their techniques and styles over the years.

As they walk through the museum's rooms, Louis and Camille's eyes are presented with a variety of scenes: the serene beauty of landscapes, the dynamism of urban scenes, and the introspection of portraits. Each work seems to carry a story, an emotion, a glimpse of the artist's unique vision.

Looking at these paintings, the writer feels as if he is witnessing a silent dialog between the artists and their canvases. Each brushstroke seems to tell a story, a part of the creative and emotional journey of the person who created it. The experience is like leafing through the pages of a visual diary, a collection of moments eternalized through art.

And so the three of them explore the museum's galleries, witnessing the works that shaped the Impressionist movement.

The painter invites the couple to visit his house nearby. When they arrive, Camille feels enchanted when she sees the lush garden that stretches out in front of them. The vibrant green of the leaves, the vivid colors of the flowers and the serenity of the environment create a magical and enveloping atmosphere.

Claude Monet's house is a mixture of soft colors and charming details, reflecting the artist's aesthetic taste. The pastel walls contrast with the white *windows, creating a feeling of lightness and harmony. Walking through the interior of the house, Luiz and Camille can feel Monet's presence in every corner, as if his passion for art were impregnated in the walls.*

In the garden, Camille feels as if she has stepped into a living painting. His garden is a symphony of colors and shapes, where the flowers dance to the rhythm of the wind. The carefully designed lines and organized beds reflect the artist's meticulous attention to detail. Walking along the stone paths, she is enchanted by the lilies that float gracefully on the water of the lake, capturing the vision that inspired countless of his paintings.

All three of them stop at the edge of the lake and their gazes turn to a picturesque bridge that spans the water. It is the famous bridge from one of Monet's iconic paintings, which depicts exactly this scene. The bridge projects like a graceful arch, punctuating the landscape with its elegance. The water reflects the sunlight in a mesmerizing way, creating a spectacle of colors and reflections. The painter smiles when he sees the admiration in Camille and Luiz's eyes.

Then Luiz and Camille follow Monet to his house in that impressionist reality. As they enter the space, their eyes light up at the dazzling sight of a palette of bright, vibrant colors that spread through every corner of the house. The walls are adorned with paintings that emanate a sense of life and movement, while the furniture and decorative objects reflect the painter's artistic personality. The atmosphere is as if the art itself had come to life and become part of the environment.

Curious, Luiz doesn't miss the opportunity to ask the artist how he got to Giverny and why he chose such a unique place to live and create. The painter, with a nostalgic smile, shares some of the remarkable episodes in his life that led him there. As Monet begins to speak, a magical effect seems to take over the space, and flashbacks of the painter's memories begin to unfold before the eyes of the three of them.

Monet takes Luiz and Camille back in time to 1872, when he painted the iconic work "Impression, Sunrise". The painting, which depicts a landscape of Le Havre, was shown at the first Impressionist exhibition in 1874 and gave rise to the movement's name. The painting captures the fleetingness of colors and light, encapsulating the core of the Impressionist approach.

The painter also talks about the creation of "Woman with a Parasol" in 1875, a piece that won him worldwide recognition and became one of the highlights of his career.

Monet reveals the challenges and inspirations behind this masterpiece, showing how each brushstroke was carefully chosen to capture the essence of the moment portrayed.

In addition, the impressionist artist shares some of the moments that marked his life until he came to Giverny. He mentions moving to Paris with his family in 1878 due to financial difficulties and the birth of his second son, Michel. However, Monet also reveals an amorous episode in his personal life: during a vacation with the Hoschédé couple, he fell in love with Alice, Mr. Hoschédé's wife. Shortly afterward, his beloved Camille Doncieux died at the age of thirty-two, leaving a deep void in his heart. Even today, the painter cannot come to terms with his wife's death at such a young age.

Monet's journey takes him to 1883 when he finally decides to move to Giverny in Normandy. It is then that the magic of the place intertwines with the painter's story, and the three friends find themselves at the epicenter of his creative journey. The garden they admire would become the setting for some of Monet's most iconic works, and the house would become his artistic sanctuary and personal refuge.

After sharing memories of his visit to Giverny, Claude invites the couple to settle down on the comfortable sofa. With a kind gesture, he promises to bring something for them to drink and enjoy while they continue their conversation. Camille and Luiz follow his instructions and settle down on the sofa, looking around the house that seems to have been painted in the same bright, cheerful colors that Monet so loved to portray on his canvases.

While they wait, Luiz can't contain his anxiety and turns to Camille, his words coming out in an excited whisper:

"Now do you believe what I've told you? I know it's a bit absurd..."

Camille, looking at Luiz with a mixture of affection and understanding, places her hand gently on his and says:

"Of course, Luiz. I've always believed in you. I just found it all so unprecedented, so out of the ordinary."

Camille's gaze turns to the space around her as if absorbing every detail of this extraordinary moment. She recognizes that, although fantastic, this experience is unique and rare. With a smile, she turns to Luiz and confides:

"This is, without a doubt, the best day of my life. Nothing compares to what I'm experiencing today."

The intensity of this moment is palpable, a fusion between the real world and the impressionist world that they have witnessed and now share

As they wait, the silence is filled with a sense of wonder and gratitude for being there, sharing this special moment alongside Monet.
The painter returns with three cups of tea, the aromatic steam from the infusion of lavender and chamomile filling the room. A simple gesture that

carries with it a touch of hospitality and attention. With a warm smile, he offers the cups to Luiz and Camille, who thank him with gestures and words of gratitude. With the soft scent of tea wafting through the air, they begin to savor each sip, a mixture of tranquility and excitement filling the moment.

Camille, curious and eager to know more about the painter and his experiences, asks Monet if he likes beaches. He nods with a nostalgic look as if those memories were brought back by the question. He begins to talk about his time on the Normandy seas, revealing a part of his life that is also marked by beauty and inspiration.

He shares how the vast expanses of ocean, the salty breeze, and the gentle sound of the waves breaking on the beach had a powerful effect on his creativity. He recalls the days when he found himself in front of the vast horizon, where the sky met the sea, an infinity of shades of blue blending together in mesmerizing harmony. The sunlight danced on the waters, creating sparkling reflections and changing colors and patterns at every moment.

In the midst of this breathtaking landscape, Monet found an inexhaustible source of inspiration. He talks about the creation of the painting "Low Tide at Pourville", and how every brushstroke he applied to the canvas was an effort to capture the ephemerality of that unique moment. The beach reveals itself as a scene of constant transformation, where the tides dictate the rhythm and nature manifests itself with ephemeral beauty.

Monet describes how he would sit by the beach, observing the fine line where the land meets the sea, the wet sand reflecting the sky and clouds with intense clarity. He sought to capture not only the appearance of the scene but also the feeling of being immersed in that environment. Each brushstroke was an effort to convey the texture of the damp sand, the gentle breeze caressing his face, and the sense of tranquility that the environment gave him.

As he speaks, Luiz and Camille are transported to that seaside setting, almost able to feel the sand beneath their feet and the salty scent of the ocean.

The painter continues to share details of his life with Luiz and Camille as if he were unveiling chapters of a book. He tells of his constant correspondence with Alice, a friendship that evolved after her husband's death in 1891. The following year, the artist and Alice united in marriage. Luiz and Camille, sitting attentively, exchange silent glances, revealing a mixture of understanding and perhaps a certain discomfort at this turning point in the painter's history.

While the words flow from Monet, emotions also dance in the air. The idea of a second marriage, especially to a woman who had previously belonged to someone else, seems to echo intriguingly in the hearts of Louis and Camille. They absorb the nuances of these life narratives, delving into the complex choices that shaped the artist's destiny.

Claude goes on to tell them about his moments of reflection in the studio, where he sought the perfect inspiration for his canvases.

The couple then sees in front of them the image of the painter thinking in his studio. He was immersed in deep thoughts to captivate the viewers in his paintings, thinking about the possibilities and how to innovate even after having painted countless remarkable paintings.

Luiz, enjoying his tea and immersed in the unique atmosphere of Monet's studio, decides to explore a little more of the painter's mind. With a curious look on his face, he turns to Monet and asks about his passions beyond painting. Monet smiles softly and replies with an air of reflection:

"I believe in traveling, my friend."

Intrigued, Luiz continues and asks about a particular place that has left a special mark on Monet. The painter, pondering for a moment, replies with a twinkle in his eye:

"It's a bit unfair to pick one place, isn't it?"

Claude lets out a light laugh, before continuing and saying:

"But if I had to mention it, I'd say that the Mediterranean region has always fascinated me."

Monet allows himself to reminisce, and his gaze seems to wander off into vivid memories:

"Antibes, Cap Martin, and the dazzling Côte d'Azur welcomed me in their enchanting colors and landscapes."

Contemplation shows on his face as he dives into the memories of those landscapes that once inspired his brushstrokes.

The conversation flows like a serene stream, and Monet reveals more about his journeys:

"London and Paris were also destinations I loved," he adds, sharing his affection for these vibrant cities. "There was so much life, culture, and movement in these places, and each visit was like discovering new nuances of life."

The couple listens attentively, immersed in the words of the painter who seems to bring his experiences to life.

After Claude finishes his recollections of his travels and remarkable places, Camille, with a curious gleam in her eyes, turns her attention to the artist's personal diary that lies in front of her. Driven by an eagerness to understand the painter's creative mind more deeply, she gently raises the question that has intrigued her for some time:

"What about the series of paintings of Rwanda Cathedral? How did you manage to capture so many variations in light and atmosphere?"

The painter, with an affectionate smile, seems to appreciate the question. He turns to Camille, his gaze taking him back to those moments of inspiration:

"Each painting in the Rwanda Cathedral series was a unique journey," he begins, "I sought to capture not only the architectural grandeur but also the way the sunlight danced over its façades at different times of the day."

He dives deeper into the explanation, sharing his meticulous approach:

"For each work, I carefully chose the time of day and the viewpoint, observing how the nuances of the light transformed the atmosphere. The secret was to observe, wait patiently, and then translate this ephemerality onto the canvas with my brushstrokes."

And as Monet speaks, the environment once again becomes a mixture of past and present. Thus showing everyone the artist is immersed in his work. The colors dance and blend, the brush strokes come to life and the paintings gradually reveal themselves under his skilled hand.

Camille, observing the scene, ends up connecting with the passion that moved him to create these iconic works. The dialog between them becomes more than just an exchange of information; it's a dive into the essence of the creative process and a deep appreciation for the ephemeral beauty of the world.

And so Monet's studio becomes a portal that transports them to the wonders of his creations and makes them feel part of that creative process.

As Monet shares his memories of creation, a new part of his artistic life emerges for the couple. The aura of the studio blends with the atmosphere of the house and garden, enveloping the three of them in a scene that looks like a moving canvas.

With a graceful gesture, Claude points to the window that reveals a panoramic view of the garden over the lake, where the emblematic Japanese bridge spans the water. The place where Luiz and Camille commented when they arrived at the artist's house was the site of a famous painting by the painter.

In this setting, he painted one of the most iconic series of his career: "Water Lilies". The mention of this series evokes a feeling of admiration, and the couple's gaze is instantly drawn to the horizon that Monet is pointing to.

The impressionist artist proudly recounts:

"Here, on this estate in Giverny, is where the ideas for the 'Water Lilies' series originated. The lake, the Japanese bridge, and the water lilies floating on the water served as an inexhaustible source of inspiration for painting."

The painter describes the beauty of his creations in the series:

"In painting the 'Water Lilies', I wanted to capture the ephemerality and serenity of nature, especially in autumn, when the flowers fall over the lake, forming a blanket of colors. The technique I used, seen as peculiar by many at the time, came to life on the canvas. When you step back, the details reveal themselves, as if the painting were coming to life before your eyes."

Words in Ink and Paper

After his words echoed in the air like strings, Monet rose from the sofa, realizing that tea time was over. With a welcoming gesture, he invites Luiz and Camille to accompany him on a stroll through the lush garden that surrounds them. As the trio head out of the house, their gaze is captured by the stunning landscape of the Giverny garden, which seems to have been modeled directly on one of Monet's own paintings.

Sunlight dances on the vibrant colors of the flowers, creating a visual spectacle that leaves the couple speechless. The magic of nature seems intertwined with Monet's artistic vision, and they find themselves immersed in a world that transcends time and reality.

In a low tone of voice, Monet shares the essence of his life:

"This garden is my life now. After facing difficult times of illness, this is where I found refuge and inspiration."

Intrigued, Luiz can't help but ask:

"Why, Claude?"

The painter looks at the horizon and says:

"My eyesight has weakened," he confesses sincerely, "The many days I spent painting outdoors in the intense sunshine have taken their toll on my eyes."

The artist reveals that, even in the face of this adversity, he didn't give in to the darkness that threatened to cloud his vision:

"I kept painting," he says with determination, "I adopted stronger strokes and bolder colors, like red, to express what I felt. The act of creating was a force that pushed me forward."

For a moment, Mancini shifts his gaze to Monet's personal diary, where an emotional passage is recorded: "I feel that everything is falling apart, my eyesight and everything else, and I'm no longer able to do anything worthwhile." He stares at Claude, connecting the written words with the narrated story, and speaks understanding the deeper meaning of those words:

"That's why you wrote it."

He shares, in a voice laden with emotion, that even after undergoing cataract surgery that brought some relief to his vision, time had run out for him:

"My time was approaching, an inescapable truth when lung cancer cast its shadow over me."

The specter of lung cancer manifested itself, bringing with it the inevitable end of his earthly existence.

The news fell over the room like a heavy shadow, and Camille looked at Luiz with a surprised expression, as if the veils that separated life and death were intertwining before her.

Mancini, feeling the urgency of curiosity, breaks the silence:

"But how is that possible, Claude? You were buried, my friend."

Disbelief permeates his words, contrasting with the almost ethereal feel of the conversation.

The painter replies with an enigmatic smile:

"Yes, physically I was buried, but a part of me seems to have found a home in that diary."

He gently points to the notebook containing his most intimate words, the ones he never intended to share:

"My innermost thoughts, my hidden concerns, and matters I would never wish to be known by others are trapped here, between these pages."

Camille and Luiz's eyes fixate on the diary, now transformed into an artifact that transcends time and reality. Understanding hangs in the air, and they absorb the impact of these profound revelations

The painter reveals a link between the ancient world and the present. Then he speaks:

"That's why," he continues, "I'm still present here and that's why you're talking to me now."

Under the serene Giverny sky, the three of them continue to walk the paths of the garden, whose colors and fragrances seem to take on a life of their own. Monet, with a mixture of serenity and melancholy, leads the way. The air carries a unique aura, a sense that something greater is at play.

An instant's pause ensues and, with eyes full of sincerity, Luiz breaks the silence that surrounds them:

"How can I help you? Is there anything I can do?"

The words fall like stones into a calm lake, creating ripples of emotion and pondering. The atmosphere is charged with a weight, a responsibility that transcends the moment. Camille, Luiz, and Monet find themselves immersed in an unexpected dilemma, a choice that could shape the painter's destiny. He explains that he believes that by freeing himself from the attachment to the words and memories contained in the diary, he will find the peace he needs to move forward

The shadows lengthen as dusk approaches, creating an atmosphere full of expectation. Mancini, with a determined look, breaks the silence that hung over them:

"How and where would you like us to do this?"

Claude replies with thoughtful serenity, pointing beyond the horizon:

"The lake here at home is no good, go to the banks of the River Seine here in Giverny."

Everything is clear, but the task ahead is permeated by a gravity that is felt by everyone. The painter offers specific instructions, suggesting that the inside pages of the diary be burned before immersing them in the waters of the river. Every word carries a weight, every secret and private story is like a prison to him.

The writer absorbs his instructions, while his mind turns to the journey he is about to undertake. He looks at the painter with a mixture of respect and compassion, feeling touched by the responsibility entrusted to him, he speaks:

"All right, I'll set you free."

Luiz places his hand on Monet's shoulder, conveying silent support, a promise to carry out the task with respect and integrity.

Camille, next to Luiz, expresses her support with a look of solidarity and determination. Together, the three embark on the last stage of their journey.

By the time they reach the riverbank, the scenery unfolds before them like a perfectly painted picture. The light of the setting sun bathes the landscape in golden hues, creating a magical and serene atmosphere. The lush nature and the tranquillity of the river's waters create a bucolic atmosphere where time seems suspended, allowing the moment to take on a unique and profound meaning.

With the sun already setting, the sky becomes a palette of vibrant colors, reflected in the calm waters of the river. The gentle breeze caresses your skin, while the sounds of nature envelop the air around you. The banks of the river are adorned with shrubs and flowers that add a touch of magic to the scene.

Luiz, with a determined gesture, pulls a lighter from his bag, and Camille holds the diary in her hands. The moment of farewell is about to happen, and the action they are about to take seems charged with meaning and emotion. Luiz lights the lighter and, one by one, the pages of the diary begin to turn to ash.

As the pages burn, the impressionist reality that surrounds them begins to disappear. The soft contours and vibrant colors that characterized their journey together begin to dissipate, giving way to the image of a sharper, more realistic world. Each flame that consumes the pages is like a link being broken, a connection being undone.

After all the pages of the diary have been consumed by the fire, reality begins to return to its normal state. However, their surroundings still seem to be imbued with the impressionistic aura that enveloped them during this unique encounter. The bright colors and soft contours seem to fade gradually, giving way to everyday reality, but something in the air remains, a sense of connection with the past.

Mancini holds the small piece of leather left over from the diary in his hands, feeling its texture between his fingers. His gaze turns to Monet, whose figure is still there in front of them, albeit in an ethereal form. With a mixture of emotions, Luiz stares at the painter and, in a voice full of sincerity, speaks:

"So long, Claude, my friend. I hope you find the peace and happiness you deserve."

The painter, with a gentle smile on his lips, replies:

"Thank you, Luiz. I wish you both much happiness."

The exchange of words between them carries a deep sense of farewell and gratitude as if they were saying goodbye to a dear friend who was present at a crucial moment in their lives.

Luiz lifts the piece of notebook and, with a determined movement, throws it into the current of the Seine. As the fragment of leather sinks and disappears beneath the surface of the water, Monet's figure begins to fade slowly, like a dream dissipating at dawn. The sensation is bittersweet, a mixture of loss and relief, as if a chapter were closing and weight were lifted from one's shoulders.

With Monet gone, the River Seine continues to flow, carrying with it the final traces of this unique journey. Luiz feels a mixture of emotions, a sense of closure, and a new beginning at the same time. The connection with the past seems to have been released, leaving room for the present and the future. As the sun sets over the horizon, Luiz and Camille remain on the riverbank, contemplating the waters of the river.

In this way, the two leave the enchanted atmosphere of Giverny and return to Giverny station, where the onset of night begins to set in. The surroundings are immersed in a peaceful calm as they wait for the train that will take them back. When the train arrives, they board, bringing with them the vivid memories of that unique journey.

Throughout the journey back, the scenery passing in front of the window is transformed by the darkness of night. The forests become mysterious shadows, while lights punctuate the houses and towns they pass through. The night sky unfolds before them, a starry blanket adorned by the crescent moon, illuminating the landscape with its soft glow.

While the train moves forward, Camille holds Luiz's hand tightly, creating a bond between them that goes beyond words. Luiz, for his part, turns his gaze to the window, immersed in contemplation. His eyes scan the rapidly sliding landscapes, absorbing every detail, as if he wanted to remember every step of the way back.

Halfway along the route, Luiz picks up his notebook and a pen, feeling the impulse to record his emotions and experiences of being with Monet. The words flow from his mind onto the paper, an attempt to capture the magic and depth of that encounter. Each stroke of the pen is like a reflection of the impact the journey has had on his soul, a transformation that resonates within him.

While night embraces the landscape, Luiz continues to write, losing himself in the words that flow freely. The return trip becomes a moment of reflection, of assimilating what has been experienced and expressing his connection with that impressionist world that seemed to exist beyond time and reality.

Luiz and Camille return to Paris, bringing with them the rich memories of their unforgettable journey. Time continues to flow like a constant river, and they resume their routine in the city. They stay at the hotel and, over the next few days, stroll through the iconic streets, soaking up the atmosphere of the City of Light. The energy of the meeting with Monet seems to continue to echo within them, infusing their everyday experiences with a new glow.

Gradually, Luiz's stay at the Hotel Ritz comes to an end, with just one week left. In the meantime, he senses an internal transformation taking place. A decision begins to take shape in his mind, gaining strength with every memory of his journey with Monet. He takes courage and calls his parents in Brazil, sharing some surprising news: he has decided that he will no longer return to his homeland. The tone of conviction in his voice is undeniable as if he had finally found what he was looking for.

With the determination of a man who has seen beyond the veil of reality, Luiz decides to sell his apartment and all his belongings in Brazil. He feels that his real journey is just beginning, and he is willing to leave behind what kept him tied to the past.

Even as Luiz's stay at the Ritz hotel comes to an end, he and Camille consolidate their relationship, which has grown through their shared experiences. A deep connection forms between them, based on a mutual understanding and a journey that transcends the ordinary. With the determination to live an authentic life in line with their aspirations, Luiz and Camille make a decision: they move in together in a charming apartment near the Luxembourg Gardens.

Mancini plunges headlong into his new life in Paris. The narrow streets and picturesque cafés become his muse, and his passion for writing only intensifies. He becomes a tireless writer, his ideas flowing like ink on paper. Each page is a window into his creative mind, each word a reflection of his restless soul. He writes as if he can't contain the avalanche of thoughts that drives him.

As Luiz navigates his way through letters, life is also writing its own story. Camille, the French woman with whom he shared the Impressionist journey, *becomes more than a fleeting memory. What began as a search for inspiration evolved into something much deeper and more meaningful. The couple find love in each other, and their lives intertwine in unexpected ways.*

Lonely days turn into shared moments, and Luiz's commitment to writing finds a balance with his love for Camille. They embark on a new adventure together, sealing their commitment with a marriage that celebrates the fusion of cultures and souls.

The writer continues to write with fervor, his passion for the art of words undiminished. Years of dedication culminate in a work that he believes is worthy of sharing with the world. He publishes his book, submitting his words and ideas to society's critical eye.

The reception is more than he could have hoped for. Critics hail him as a talented and promising author, and people connect with the stories he has woven. The pages he has spent so long crafting take on a life of their own in the hands of readers. The success of his book is a validation of his journey, a testament to his quest for authenticity and his passion for expression.

However, readers wonder: Was the encounter with the artist just the writer's creative delirium, a momentary escape from reality? Or is there something deeper and more mysterious behind this experience, something that transcends our common understanding?

The pages of the story bend, and the paints of the past and present blend into an intriguing picture of possibilities. And so the narrative remains in suspense, an enigma to be debated and interpreted, an invitation for each reader to draw their own lines between the real and the imaginary, between art and life, between what we know and what we may never really know.